DONALD DUCK in Burning Hearts

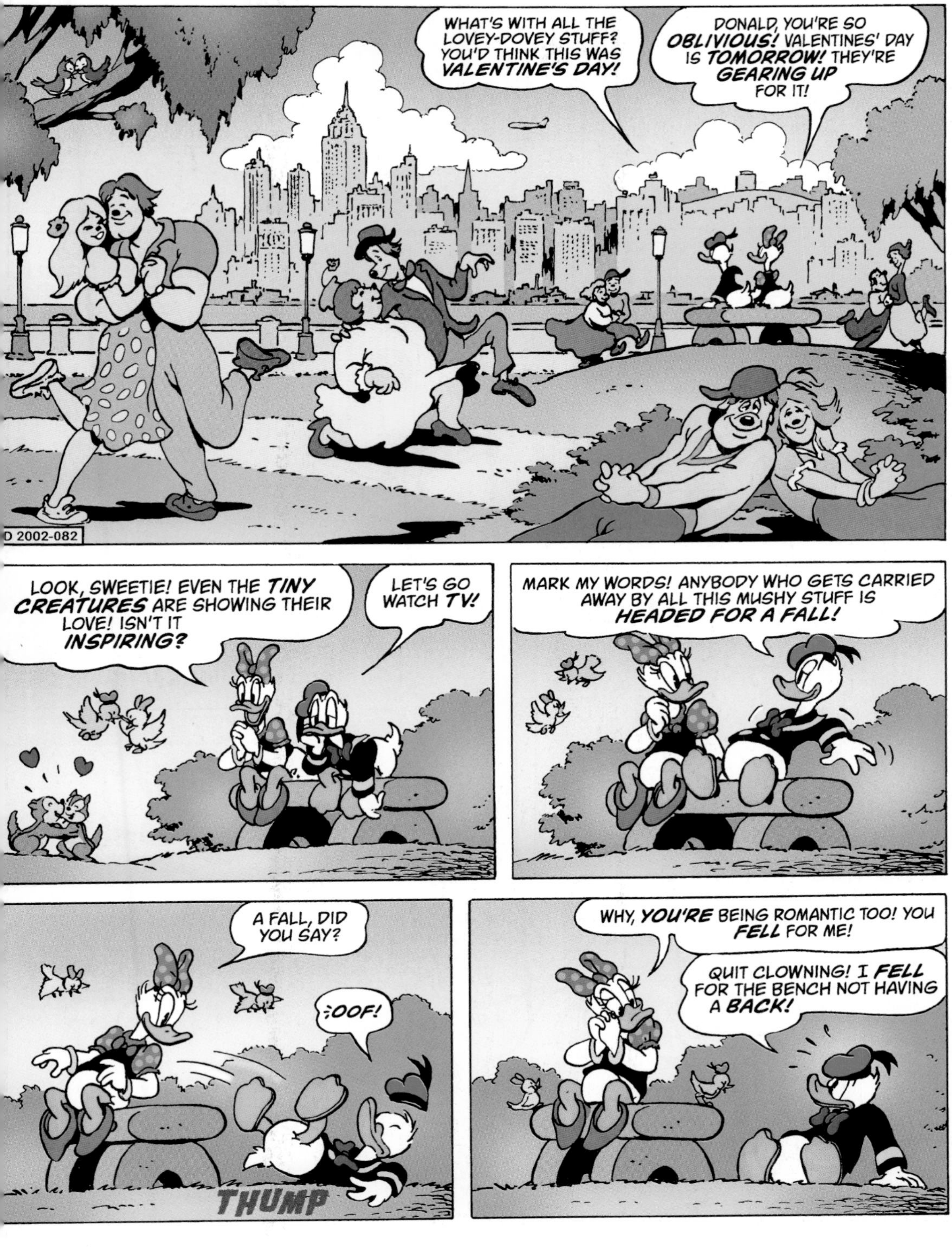
WHAT'S WITH ALL THE LOVEY-DOVEY STUFF? YOU'D THINK THIS WAS VALENTINE'S DAY!
DONALD, YOU'RE SO OBLIVIOUS! VALENTINES' DAY IS TOMORROW! THEY'RE GEARING UP FOR IT!
D 2002-082
LOOK, SWEETIE! EVEN THE TINY CREATURES ARE SHOWING THEIR LOVE! ISN'T IT INSPIRING?
LET'S GO WATCH TV!
MARK MY WORDS! ANYBODY WHO GETS CARRIED AWAY BY ALL THIS MUSHY STUFF IS HEADED FOR A FALL!
A FALL, DID YOU SAY?
OOF!
THUMP
WHY, YOU'RE BEING ROMANTIC TOO! YOU FELL FOR ME!
QUIT CLOWNING! I FELL FOR THE BENCH NOT HAVING A BACK!

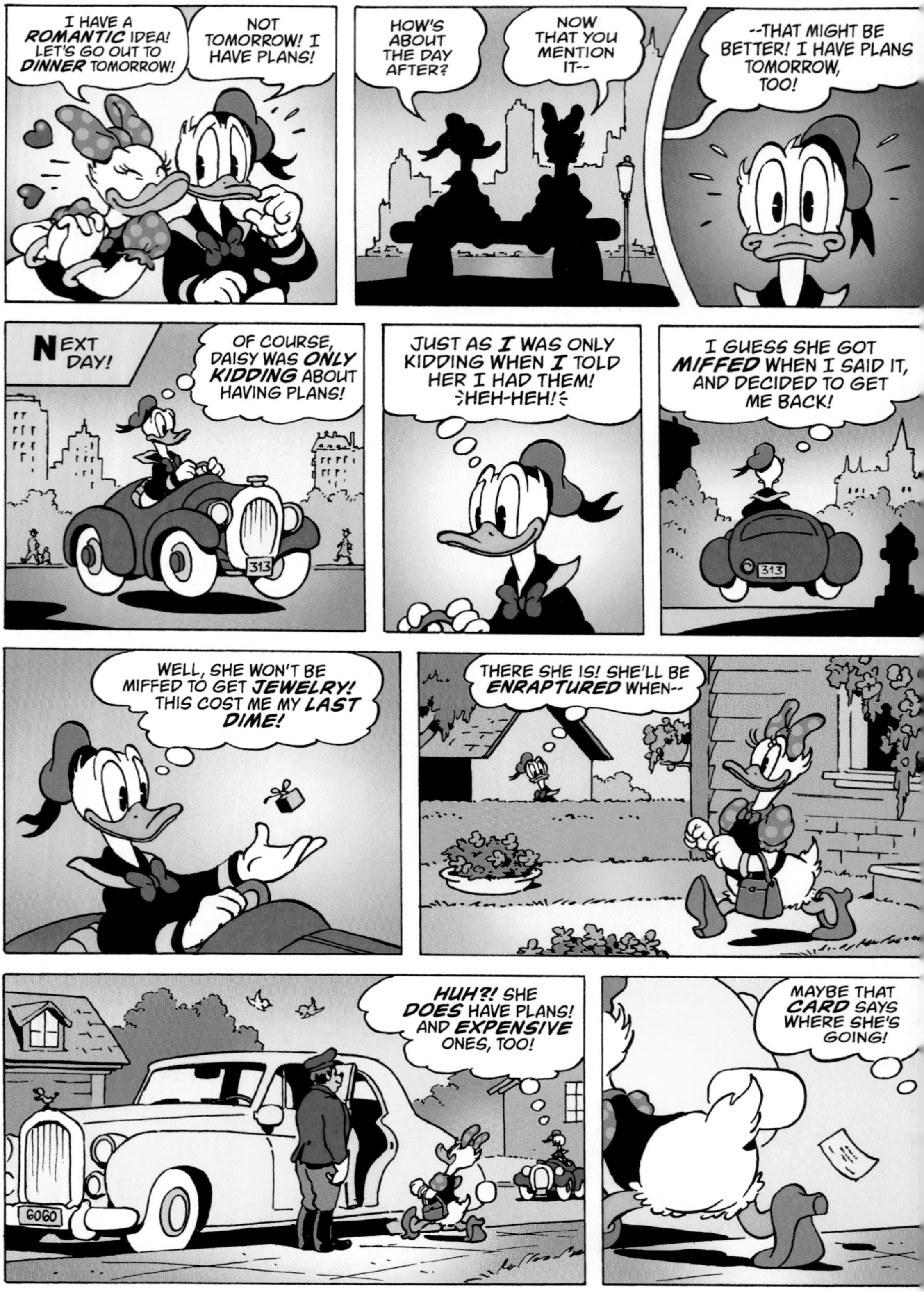
I HAVE A ROMANTIC IDEA! LET'S GO OUT TO DINNER TOMORROW!
NOT TOMORROW! I HAVE PLANS!
HOW'S ABOUT THE DAY AFTER?
NOW THAT YOU MENTION IT--
--THAT MIGHT BE BETTER! I HAVE PLANS TOMORROW, TOO!
NEXT DAY!
OF COURSE, DAISY WAS ONLY KIDDING ABOUT HAVING PLANS!
313
JUST AS I WAS ONLY KIDDING WHEN I TOLD HER I HAD THEM! HEH-HEH!
I GUESS SHE GOT MIFFED WHEN I SAID IT, AND DECIDED TO GET ME BACK!
313
WELL, SHE WON'T BE MIFFED TO GET JEWELRY! THIS COST ME MY LAST DIME!
THERE SHE IS! SHE'LL BE ENRAPTURED WHEN--
HUH?! SHE DOES HAVE PLANS! AND EXPENSIVE ONES, TOO!
6060
MAYBE THAT CARD SAYS WHERE SHE'S GOING!

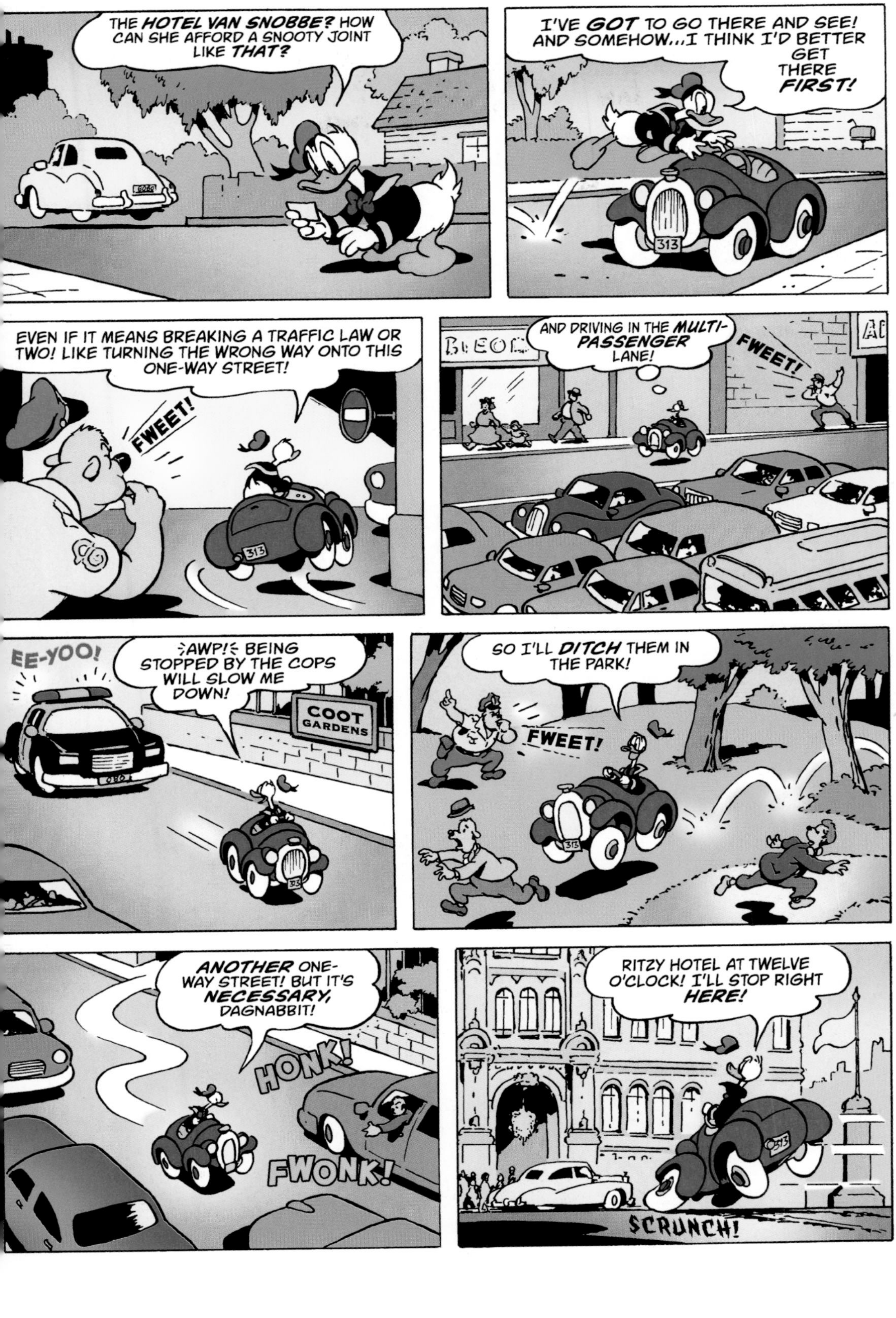
THE HOTEL VAN SNOBBE? HOW CAN SHE AFFORD A SNOOTY JOINT LIKE THAT?
I'VE GOT TO GO THERE AND SEE! AND SOMEHOW...I THINK I'D BETTER GET THERE FIRST!
EVEN IF IT MEANS BREAKING A TRAFFIC LAW OR TWO! LIKE TURNING THE WRONG WAY ONTO THIS ONE-WAY STREET!
FWEET!
AND DRIVING IN THE MULTI-PASSENGER LANE!
FWEET!
EE-YOO!
AWP! BEING STOPPED BY THE COPS WILL SLOW ME DOWN!
COOT GARDENS
SO I'LL DITCH THEM IN THE PARK!
FWEET!
ANOTHER ONE-WAY STREET! BUT IT'S NECESSARY, DAGNABBIT!
HONK!
FWONK!
RITZY HOTEL AT TWELVE O'CLOCK! I'LL STOP RIGHT HERE!
SCRUNCH!

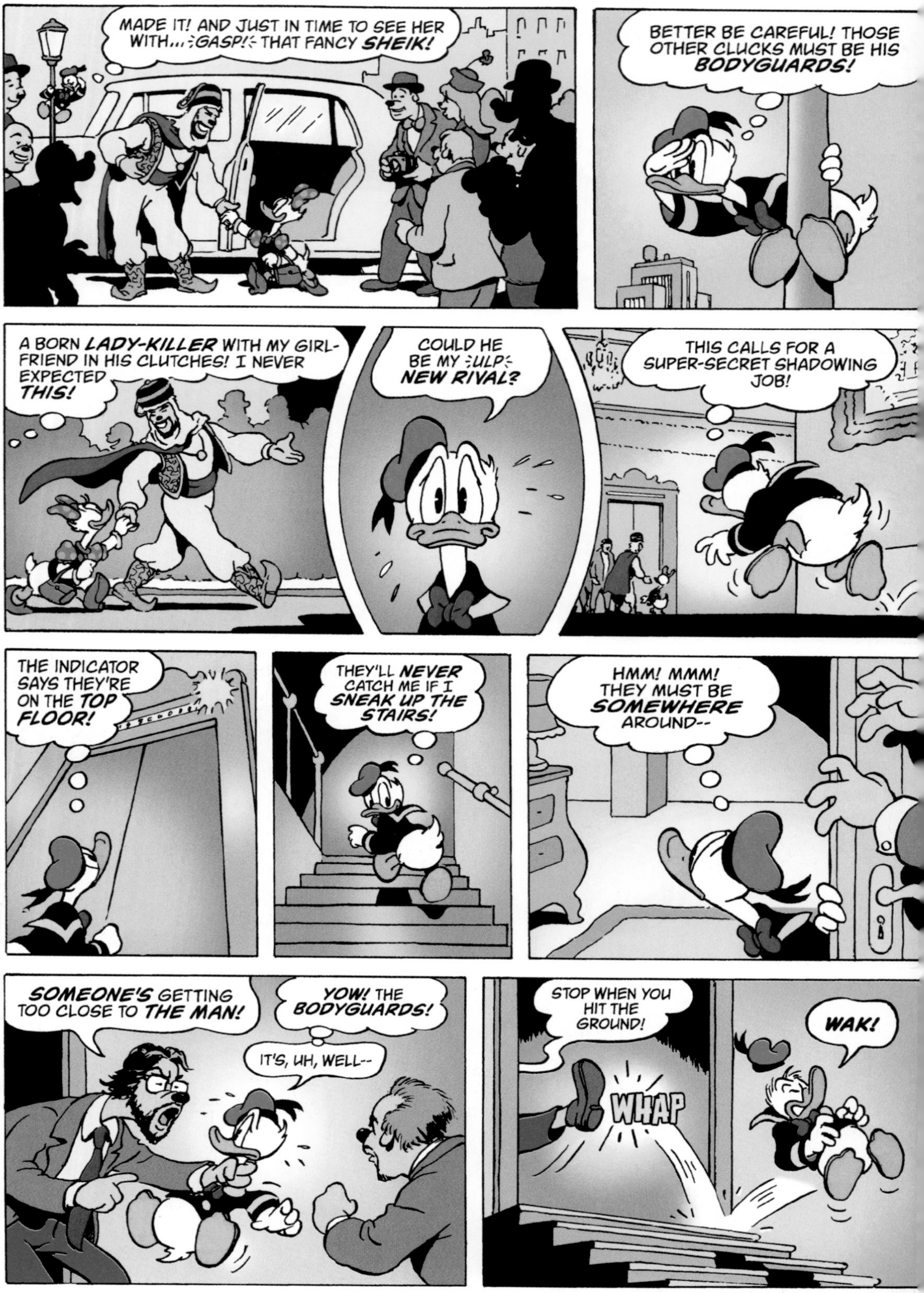

MADE IT! AND JUST IN TIME TO SEE HER WITH... GASP! THAT FANCY SHEIK!
BETTER BE CAREFUL! THOSE OTHER CLUCKS MUST BE HIS BODYGUARDS!
A BORN LADY-KILLER WITH MY GIRL-FRIEND IN HIS CLUTCHES! I NEVER EXPECTED THIS!
COULD HE BE MY ULP NEW RIVAL?
THIS CALLS FOR A SUPER-SECRET SHADOWING JOB!
THE INDICATOR SAYS THEY'RE ON THE TOP FLOOR!
THEY'LL NEVER CATCH ME IF I SNEAK UP THE STAIRS!
HMM! MMM! THEY MUST BE SOMEWHERE AROUND--
SOMEONE'S GETTING TOO CLOSE TO THE MAN!
YOW! THE BODYGUARDS!
IT'S, UH, WELL--
STOP WHEN YOU HIT THE GROUND!
WHAP
WAK!

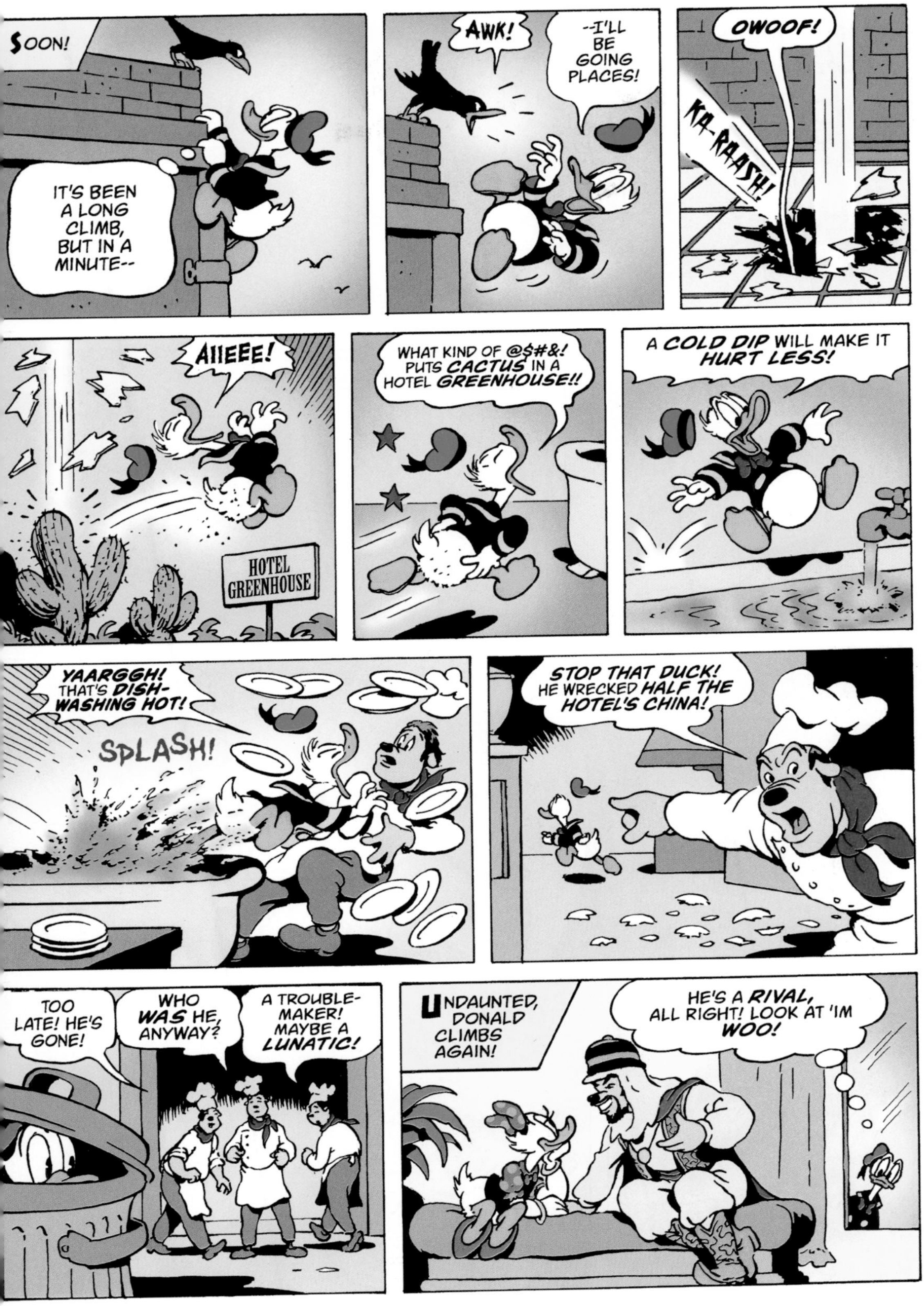
SOON!
IT'S BEEN A LONG CLIMB, BUT IN A MINUTE--
AWK!
--I'LL BE GOING PLACES!
OWOOF!
KA-RAASH!
AIIEEE!
HOTEL GREENHOUSE
WHAT KIND OF @$#&! PUTS CACTUS IN A HOTEL GREENHOUSE!!
A COLD DIP WILL MAKE IT HURT LESS!
YAARGGH! THAT'S DISH-WASHING HOT!
SPLASH!
STOP THAT DUCK! HE WRECKED HALF THE HOTEL'S CHINA!
TOO LATE! HE'S GONE!
WHO WAS HE, ANYWAY?
A TROUBLE-MAKER! MAYBE A LUNATIC!
UNDAUNTED, DONALD CLIMBS AGAIN!
HE'S A RIVAL, ALL RIGHT! LOOK AT 'IM WOO!

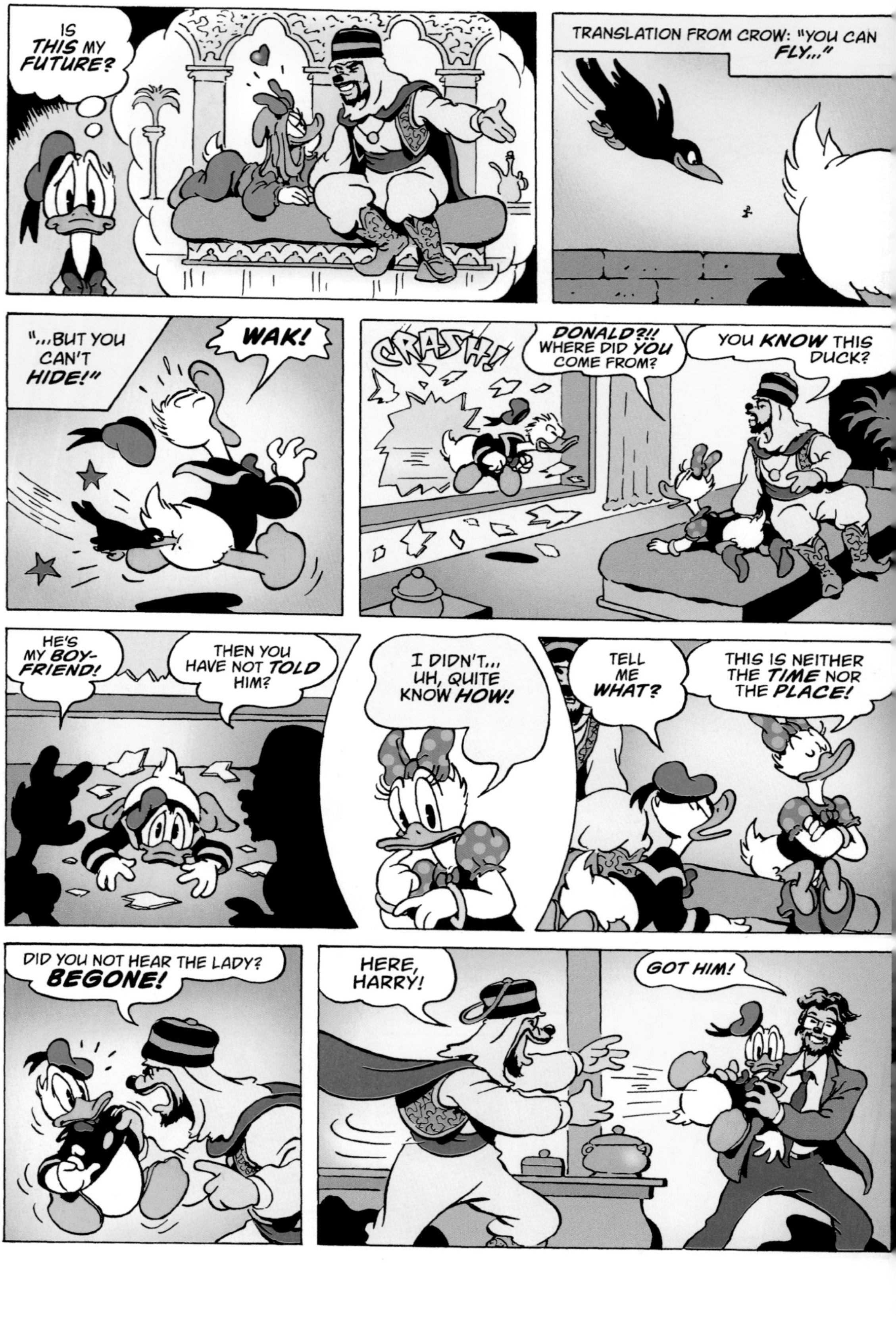

IS THIS MY FUTURE?
TRANSLATION FROM CROW: "YOU CAN FLY..."
"...BUT YOU CAN'T HIDE!"
WAK!
CRASH!
DONALD?!! WHERE DID YOU COME FROM?
YOU KNOW THIS DUCK?
HE'S MY BOY-FRIEND!
THEN YOU HAVE NOT TOLD HIM?
I DIDN'T... UH, QUITE KNOW HOW!
TELL ME WHAT?
THIS IS NEITHER THE TIME NOR THE PLACE!
DID YOU NOT HEAR THE LADY? BEGONE!
HERE, HARRY!
GOT HIM!

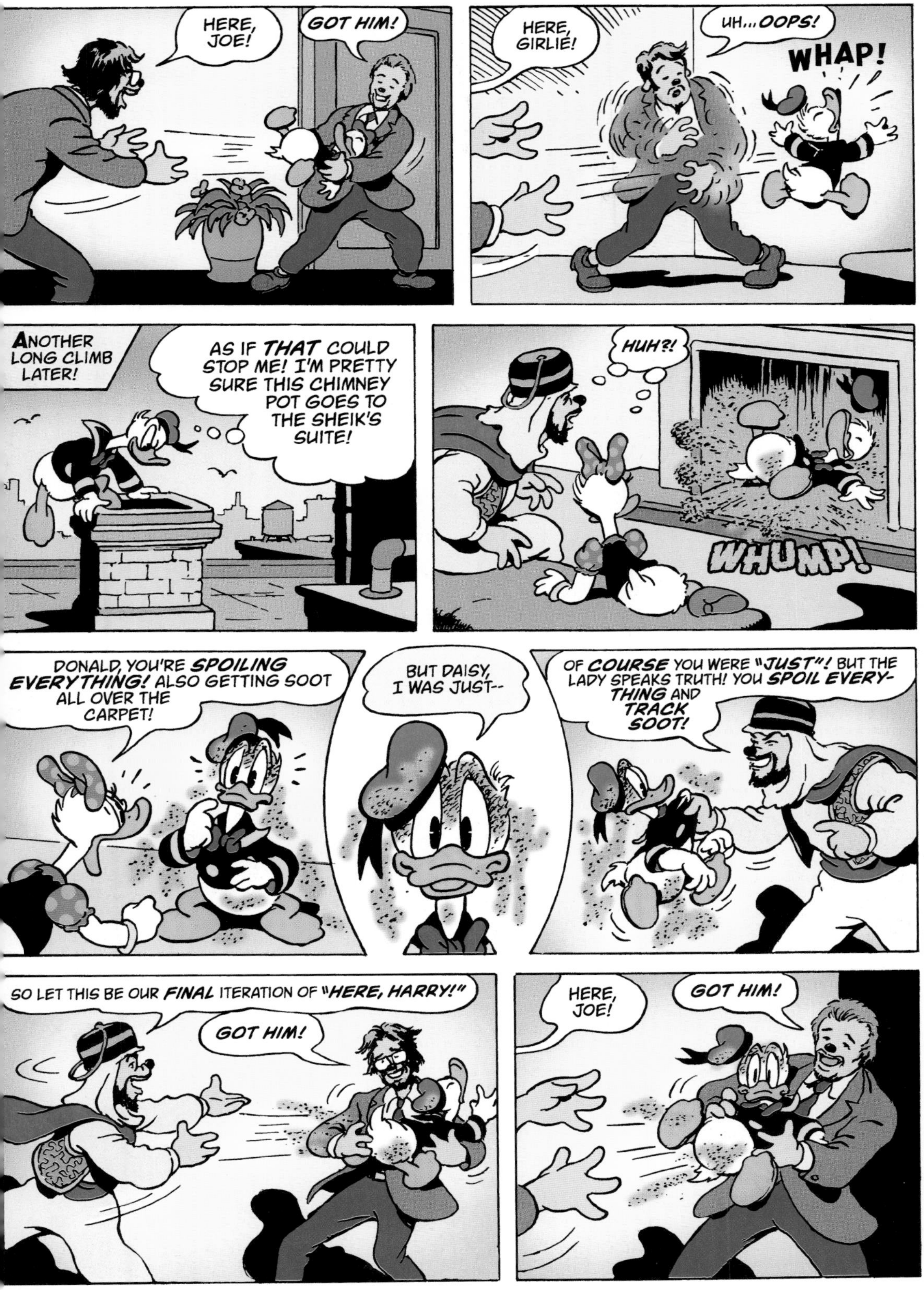
HERE, JOE!
GOT HIM!
HERE, GIRLIE!
UH... OOPS!
WHAP!
ANOTHER LONG CLIMB LATER!
AS IF THAT COULD STOP ME! I'M PRETTY SURE THIS CHIMNEY POT GOES TO THE SHEIK'S SUITE!
HUH?!
WHUMP!
DONALD, YOU'RE SPOILING EVERYTHING! ALSO GETTING SOOT ALL OVER THE CARPET!
BUT DAISY, I WAS JUST--
OF COURSE YOU WERE "JUST"! BUT THE LADY SPEAKS TRUTH! YOU SPOIL EVERY-THING AND TRACK SOOT!
SO LET THIS BE OUR FINAL ITERATION OF "HERE, HARRY!"
GOT HIM!
HERE, JOE!
GOT HIM!

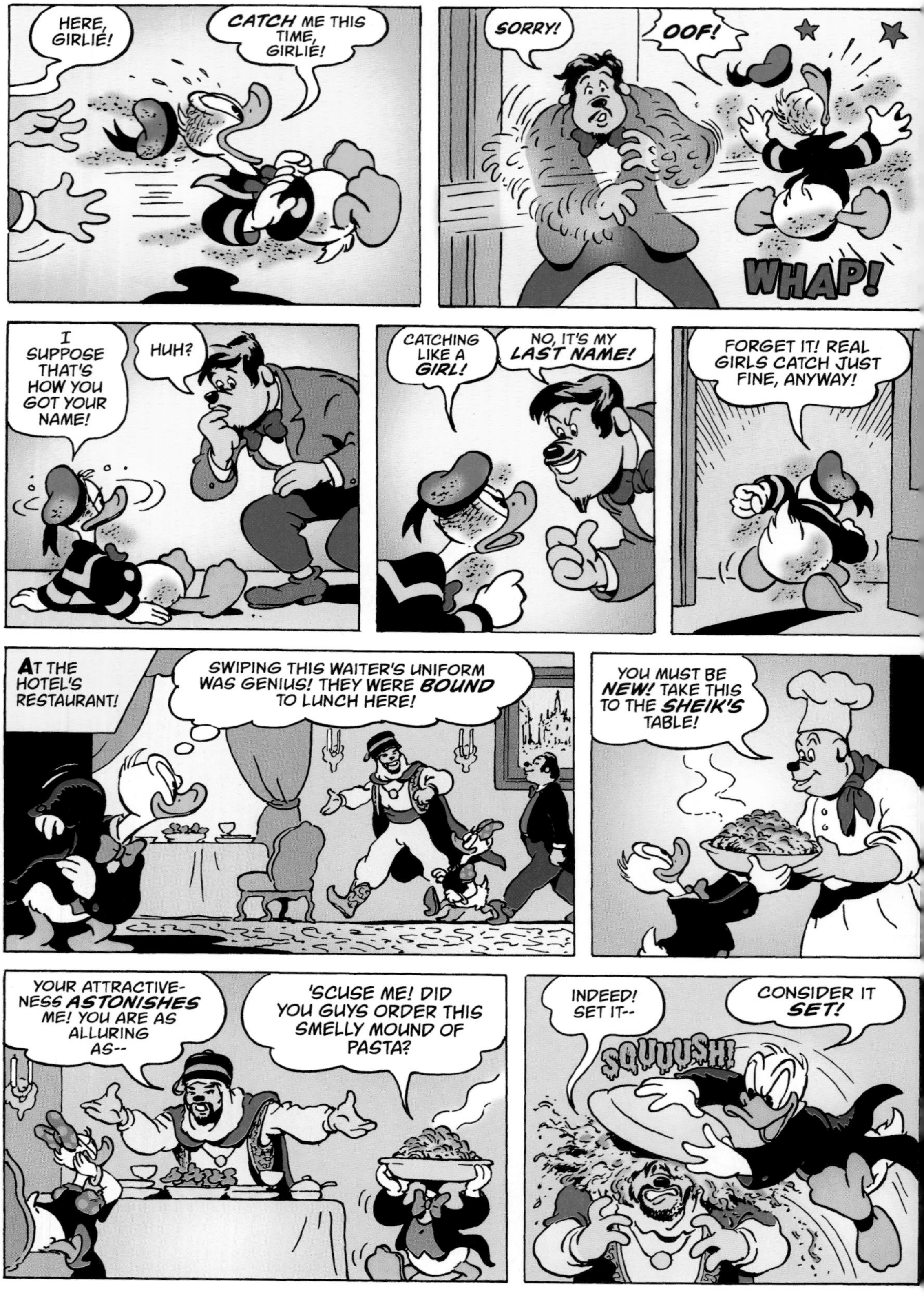

HERE, GIRLIE!
CATCH ME THIS TIME, GIRLIE!
SORRY!
OOF!
WHAP!
I SUPPOSE THAT'S HOW YOU GOT YOUR NAME!
HUH?
CATCHING LIKE A GIRL!
NO, IT'S MY LAST NAME!
FORGET IT! REAL GIRLS CATCH JUST FINE, ANYWAY!
AT THE HOTEL'S RESTAURANT!
SWIPING THIS WAITER'S UNIFORM WAS GENIUS! THEY WERE BOUND TO LUNCH HERE!
YOU MUST BE NEW! TAKE THIS TO THE SHEIK'S TABLE!
YOUR ATTRACTIVENESS ASTONISHES ME! YOU ARE AS ALLURING AS--
'SCUSE ME! DID YOU GUYS ORDER THIS SMELLY MOUND OF PASTA?
INDEED! SET IT--
CONSIDER IT SET!
SQUUUSH!

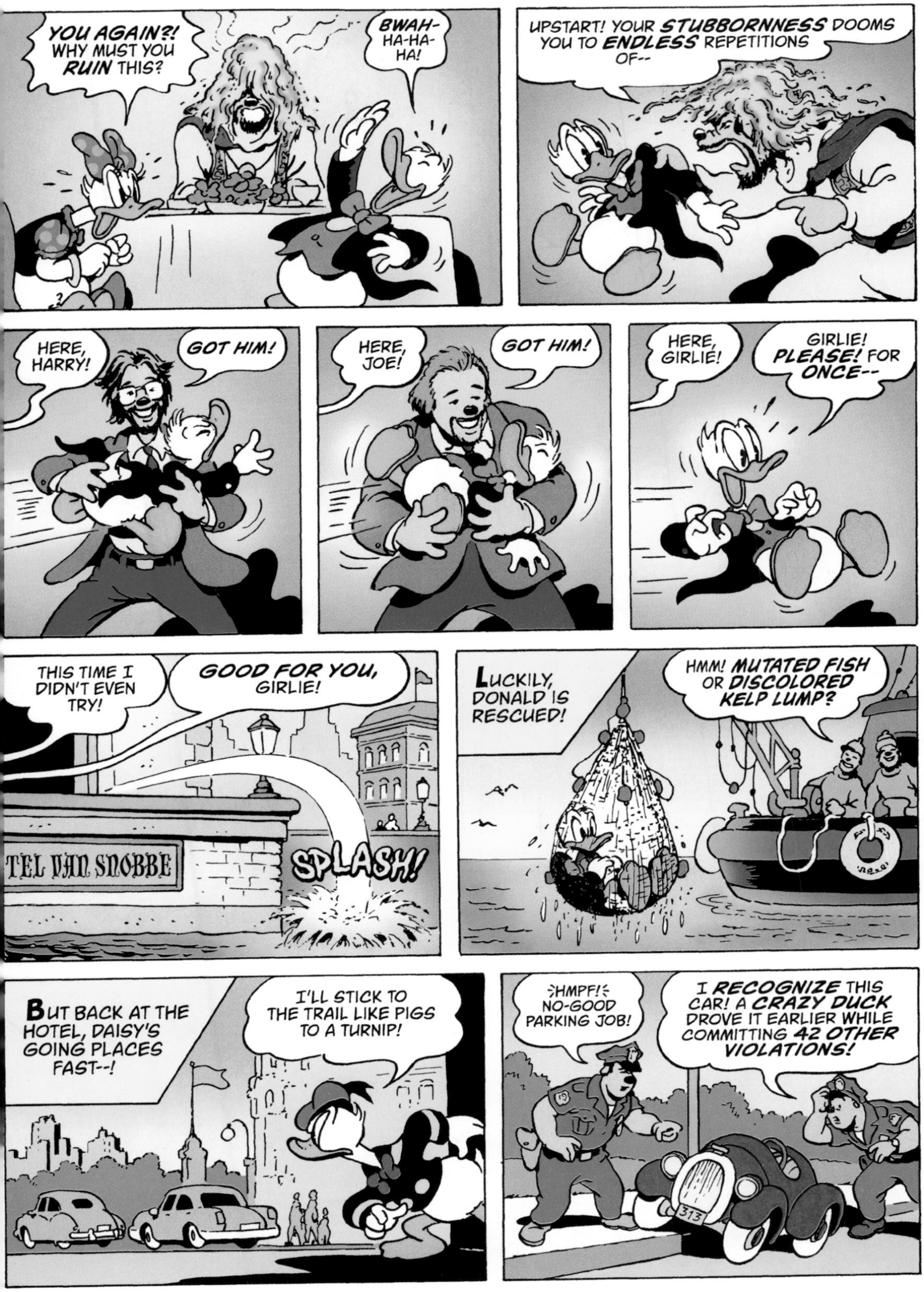

YOU AGAIN?! WHY MUST YOU RUIN THIS?
BWAH-HA-HA-HA!
UPSTART! YOUR STUBBORNNESS DOOMS YOU TO ENDLESS REPETITIONS OF--
HERE, HARRY!
GOT HIM!
HERE, JOE!
GOT HIM!
HERE, GIRLIE!
GIRLIE! PLEASE! FOR ONCE--
THIS TIME I DIDN'T EVEN TRY!
GOOD FOR YOU, GIRLIE!
TEL VAN SNOBBE
SPLASH!
LUCKILY, DONALD IS RESCUED!
HMM! MUTATED FISH OR DISCOLORED KELP LUMP?
BUT BACK AT THE HOTEL, DAISY'S GOING PLACES FAST--!
I'LL STICK TO THE TRAIL LIKE PIGS TO A TURNIP!
HMPF! NO-GOOD PARKING JOB!
I RECOGNIZE THIS CAR! A CRAZY DUCK DROVE IT EARLIER WHILE COMMITTING 42 OTHER VIOLATIONS!
313

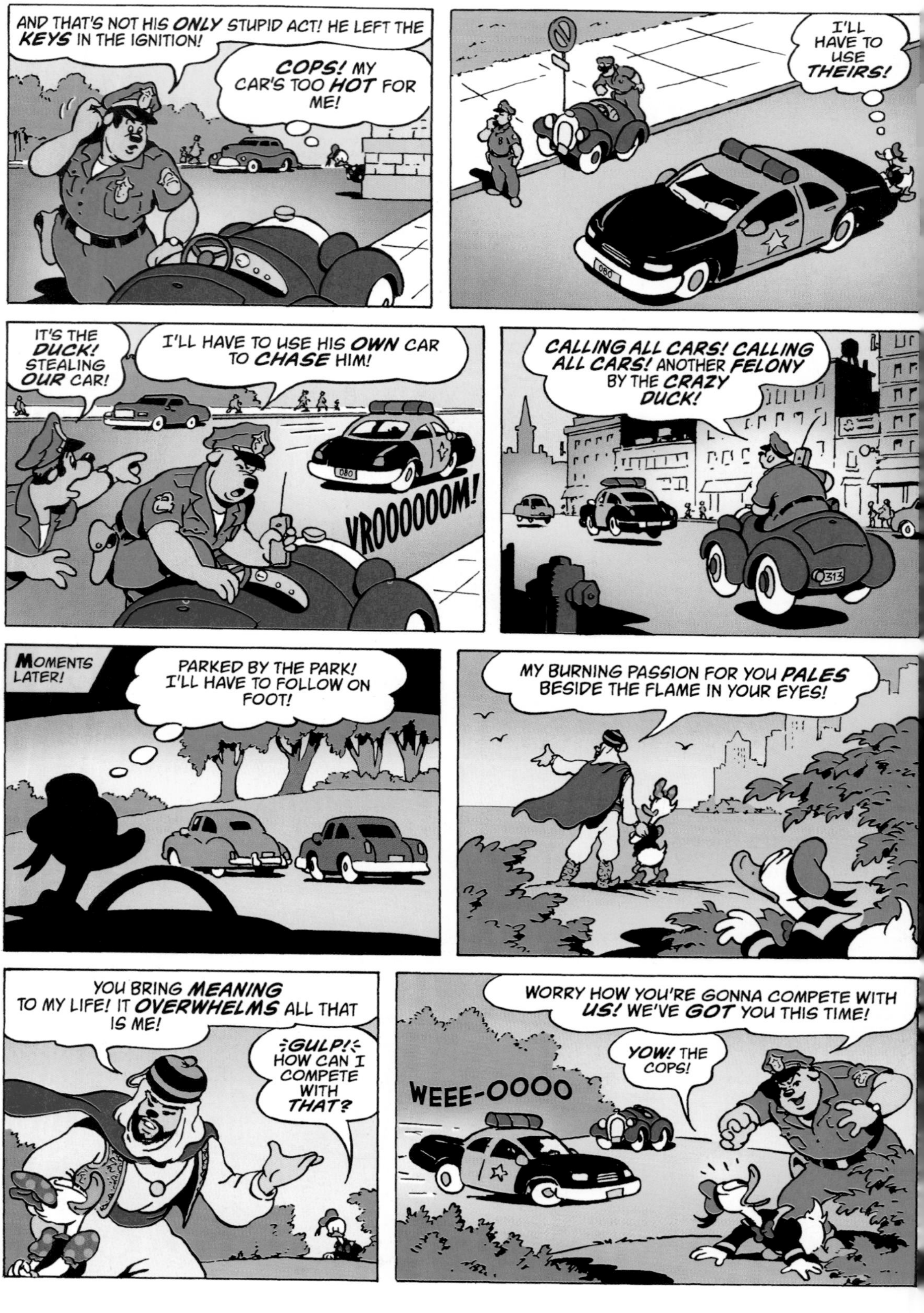
AND THAT'S NOT HIS ONLY STUPID ACT! HE LEFT THE KEYS IN THE IGNITION!
COPS! MY CAR'S TOO HOT FOR ME!
I'LL HAVE TO USE THEIRS!
IT'S THE DUCK! STEALING OUR CAR!
I'LL HAVE TO USE HIS OWN CAR TO CHASE HIM!
VROOOOOOM!
CALLING ALL CARS! CALLING ALL CARS! ANOTHER FELONY BY THE CRAZY DUCK!
MOMENTS LATER!
PARKED BY THE PARK! I'LL HAVE TO FOLLOW ON FOOT!
MY BURNING PASSION FOR YOU PALES BESIDE THE FLAME IN YOUR EYES!
YOU BRING MEANING TO MY LIFE! IT OVERWHELMS ALL THAT IS ME!
GULP! HOW CAN I COMPETE WITH THAT?
WORRY HOW YOU'RE GONNA COMPETE WITH US! WE'VE GOT YOU THIS TIME!
YOW! THE COPS!
WEEE-OOOO

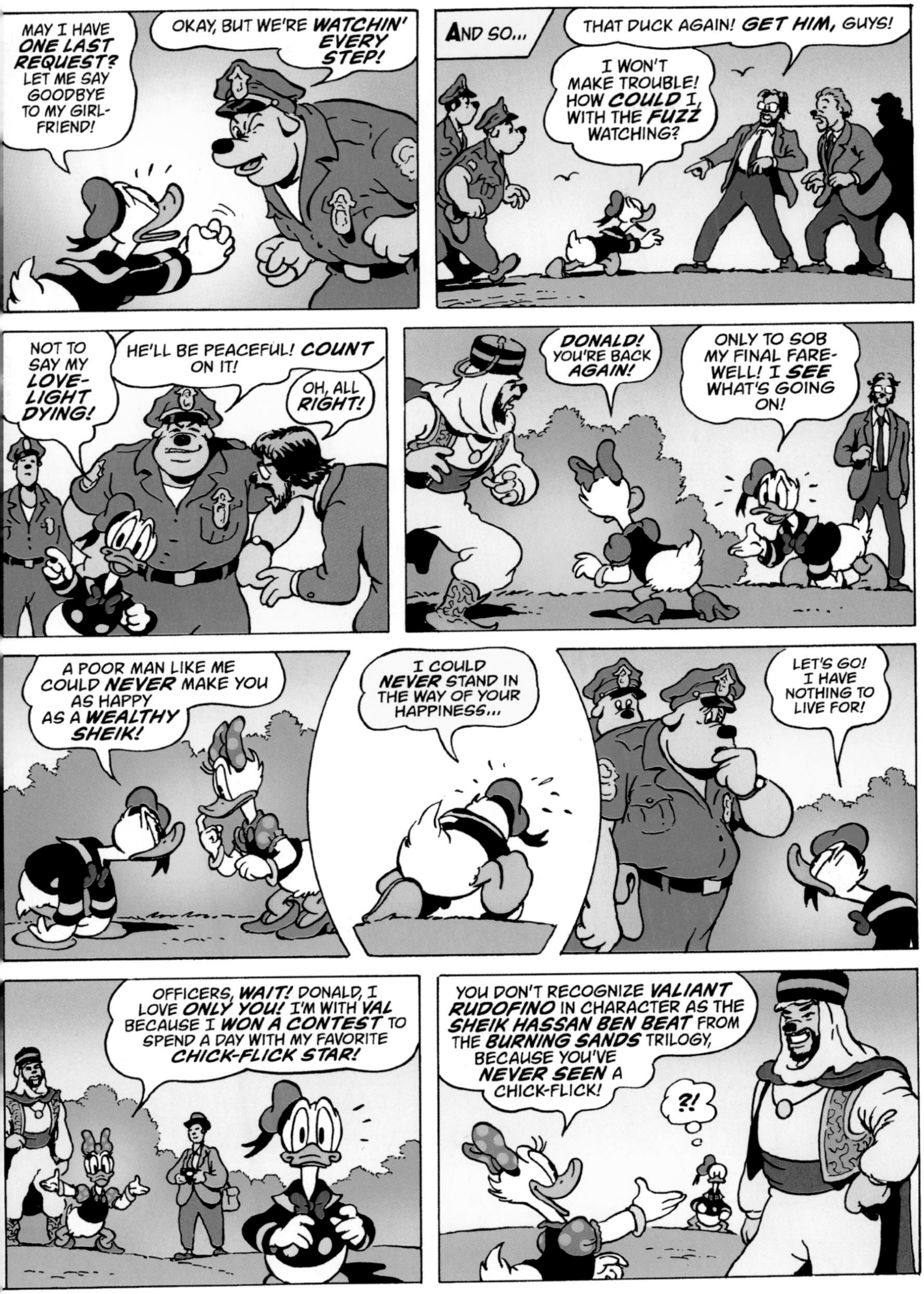
MAY I HAVE ONE LAST REQUEST? LET ME SAY GOODBYE TO MY GIRL-FRIEND!
OKAY, BUT WE'RE WATCHIN' EVERY STEP!
AND SO...
THAT DUCK AGAIN! GET HIM, GUYS!
I WON'T MAKE TROUBLE! HOW COULD I, WITH THE FUZZ WATCHING?
NOT TO SAY MY LOVE-LIGHT DYING!
HE'LL BE PEACEFUL! COUNT ON IT!
OH, ALL RIGHT!
DONALD! YOU'RE BACK AGAIN!
ONLY TO SOB MY FINAL FARE-WELL! I SEE WHAT'S GOING ON!
A POOR MAN LIKE ME COULD NEVER MAKE YOU AS HAPPY AS A WEALTHY SHEIK!
I COULD NEVER STAND IN THE WAY OF YOUR HAPPINESS...
LET'S GO! I HAVE NOTHING TO LIVE FOR!
OFFICERS, WAIT! DONALD, I LOVE ONLY YOU! I'M WITH VAL BECAUSE I WON A CONTEST TO SPEND A DAY WITH MY FAVORITE CHICK-FLICK STAR!
YOU DON'T RECOGNIZE VALIANT RUDOFINO IN CHARACTER AS THE SHEIK HASSAN BEN BEAT FROM THE BURNING SANDS TRILOGY, BECAUSE YOU'VE NEVER SEEN A CHICK-FLICK!
?!

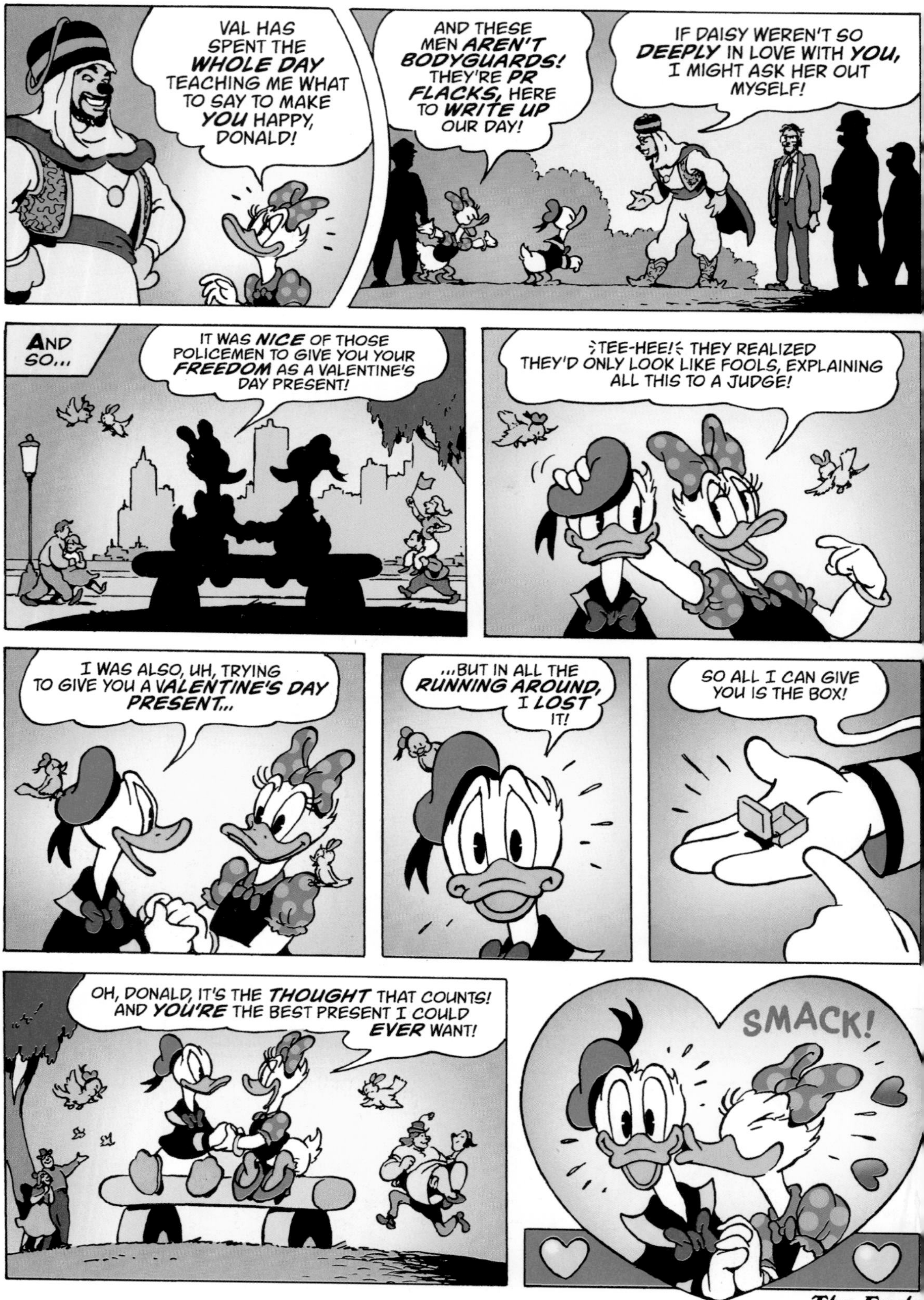
VAL HAS SPENT THE WHOLE DAY TEACHING ME WHAT TO SAY TO MAKE YOU HAPPY, DONALD!
AND THESE MEN AREN'T BODYGUARDS! THEY'RE PR FLACKS, HERE TO WRITE UP OUR DAY!
IF DAISY WEREN'T SO DEEPLY IN LOVE WITH YOU, I MIGHT ASK HER OUT MYSELF!
AND SO...
IT WAS NICE OF THOSE POLICEMEN TO GIVE YOU YOUR FREEDOM AS A VALENTINE'S DAY PRESENT!
TEE-HEE! THEY REALIZED THEY'D ONLY LOOK LIKE FOOLS, EXPLAINING ALL THIS TO A JUDGE!
I WAS ALSO, UH, TRYING TO GIVE YOU A VALENTINE'S DAY PRESENT...
...BUT IN ALL THE RUNNING AROUND, I LOST IT!
SO ALL I CAN GIVE YOU IS THE BOX!
OH, DONALD, IT'S THE THOUGHT THAT COUNTS! AND YOU'RE THE BEST PRESENT I COULD EVER WANT!
SMACK!

The End

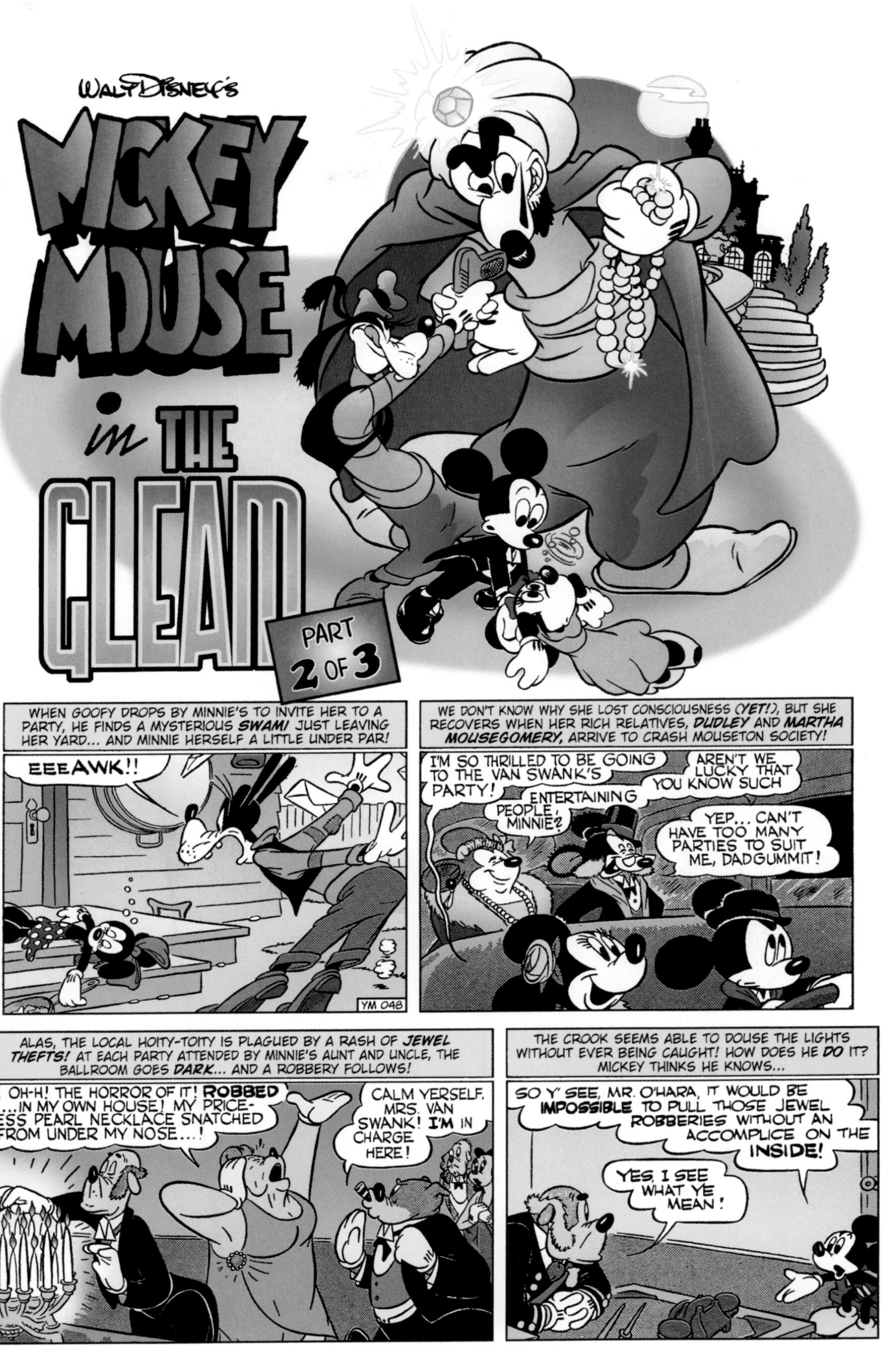

WALT DISNEY'S
MICKEY MOUSE
in THE GLEAM
PART 2 OF 3
WHEN GOOFY DROPS BY MINNIE'S TO INVITE HER TO A PARTY, HE FINDS A MYSTERIOUS SWAMI JUST LEAVING HER YARD... AND MINNIE HERSELF A LITTLE UNDER PAR!
EEEAWK!!
YM 048
WE DON'T KNOW WHY SHE LOST CONSCIOUSNESS (YET!), BUT SHE RECOVERS WHEN HER RICH RELATIVES, DUDLEY AND MARTHA MOUSEGOMERY, ARRIVE TO CRASH MOUSETON SOCIETY!
I'M SO THRILLED TO BE GOING TO THE VAN SWANK'S PARTY!
AREN'T WE LUCKY THAT YOU KNOW SUCH ENTERTAINING PEOPLE, MINNIE?
YEP... CAN'T HAVE TOO MANY PARTIES TO SUIT ME, DADGUMMIT!
ALAS, THE LOCAL HOITY-TOITY IS PLAGUED BY A RASH OF JEWEL THEFTS! AT EACH PARTY ATTENDED BY MINNIE'S AUNT AND UNCLE, THE BALLROOM GOES DARK... AND A ROBBERY FOLLOWS!
OH-H! THE HORROR OF IT! ROBBED ...IN MY OWN HOUSE! MY PRICE-LESS PEARL NECKLACE SNATCHED FROM UNDER MY NOSE...!
CALM YERSELF, MRS. VAN SWANK! I'M IN CHARGE HERE!
THE CROOK SEEMS ABLE TO DOUSE THE LIGHTS WITHOUT EVER BEING CAUGHT! HOW DOES HE DO IT? MICKEY THINKS HE KNOWS...
SO Y' SEE, MR. O'HARA, IT WOULD BE IMPOSSIBLE TO PULL THOSE JEWEL ROBBERIES WITHOUT AN ACCOMPLICE ON THE INSIDE!
YES, I SEE WHAT YE MEAN!

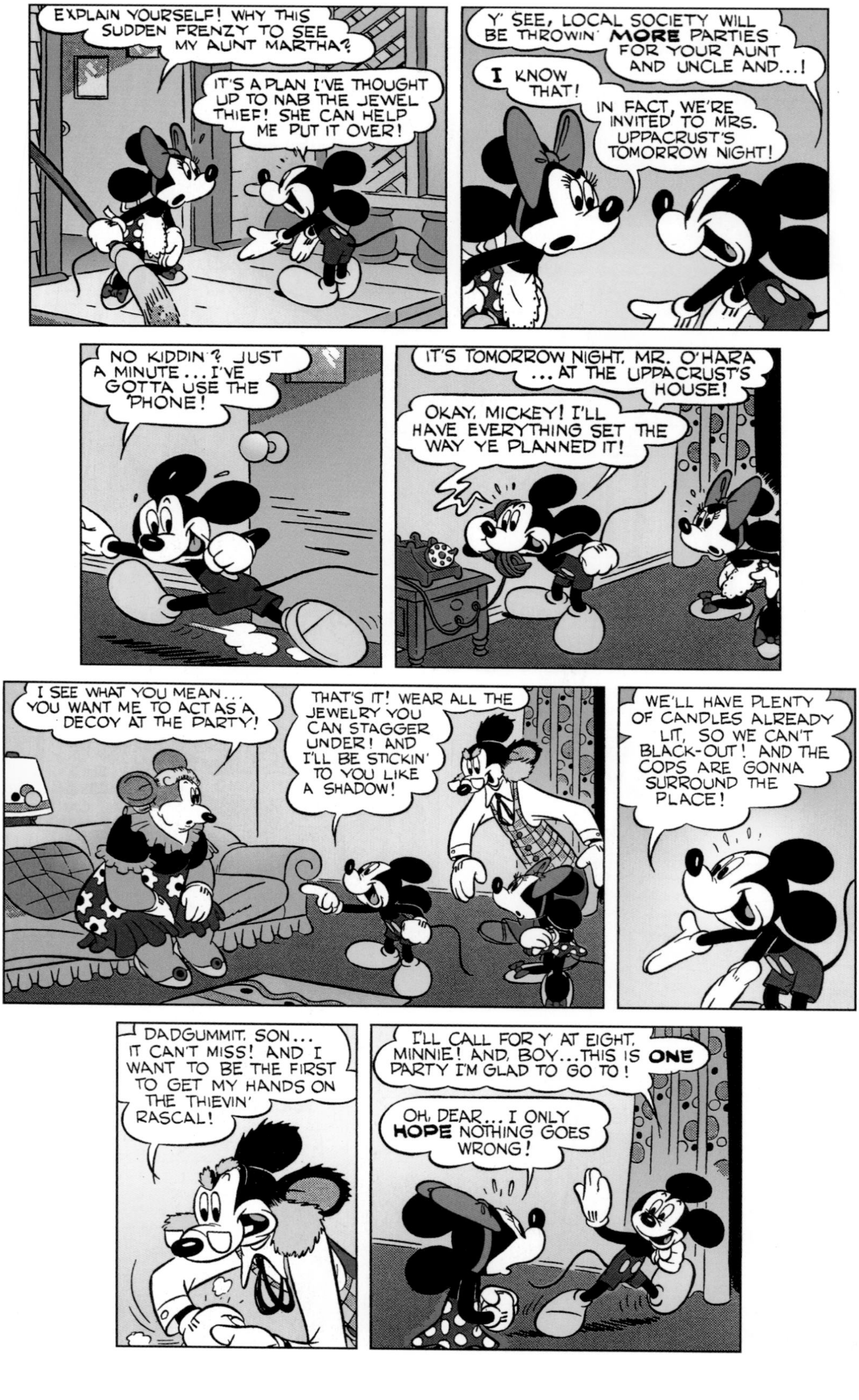
EXPLAIN YOURSELF! WHY THIS SUDDEN FRENZY TO SEE MY AUNT MARTHA?
IT'S A PLAN I'VE THOUGHT UP TO NAB THE JEWEL THIEF! SHE CAN HELP ME PUT IT OVER!
Y' SEE, LOCAL SOCIETY WILL BE THROWIN' MORE PARTIES FOR YOUR AUNT AND UNCLE AND...!
I KNOW THAT!
IN FACT, WE'RE INVITED TO MRS. UPPACRUST'S TOMORROW NIGHT!
NO KIDDIN'? JUST A MINUTE... I'VE GOTTA USE THE 'PHONE!
IT'S TOMORROW NIGHT, MR. O'HARA ... AT THE UPPACRUST'S HOUSE!
OKAY, MICKEY! I'LL HAVE EVERYTHING SET THE WAY YE PLANNED IT!
I SEE WHAT YOU MEAN... YOU WANT ME TO ACT AS A DECOY AT THE PARTY!
THAT'S IT! WEAR ALL THE JEWELRY YOU CAN STAGGER UNDER! AND I'LL BE STICKIN' TO YOU LIKE A SHADOW!
WE'LL HAVE PLENTY OF CANDLES ALREADY LIT, SO WE CAN'T BLACK-OUT! AND THE COPS ARE GONNA SURROUND THE PLACE!
DADGUMMIT, SON... IT CAN'T MISS! AND I WANT TO BE THE FIRST TO GET MY HANDS ON THE THIEVIN' RASCAL!
I'LL CALL FOR Y' AT EIGHT, MINNIE! AND, BOY... THIS IS ONE PARTY I'M GLAD TO GO TO!
OH, DEAR... I ONLY HOPE NOTHING GOES WRONG!

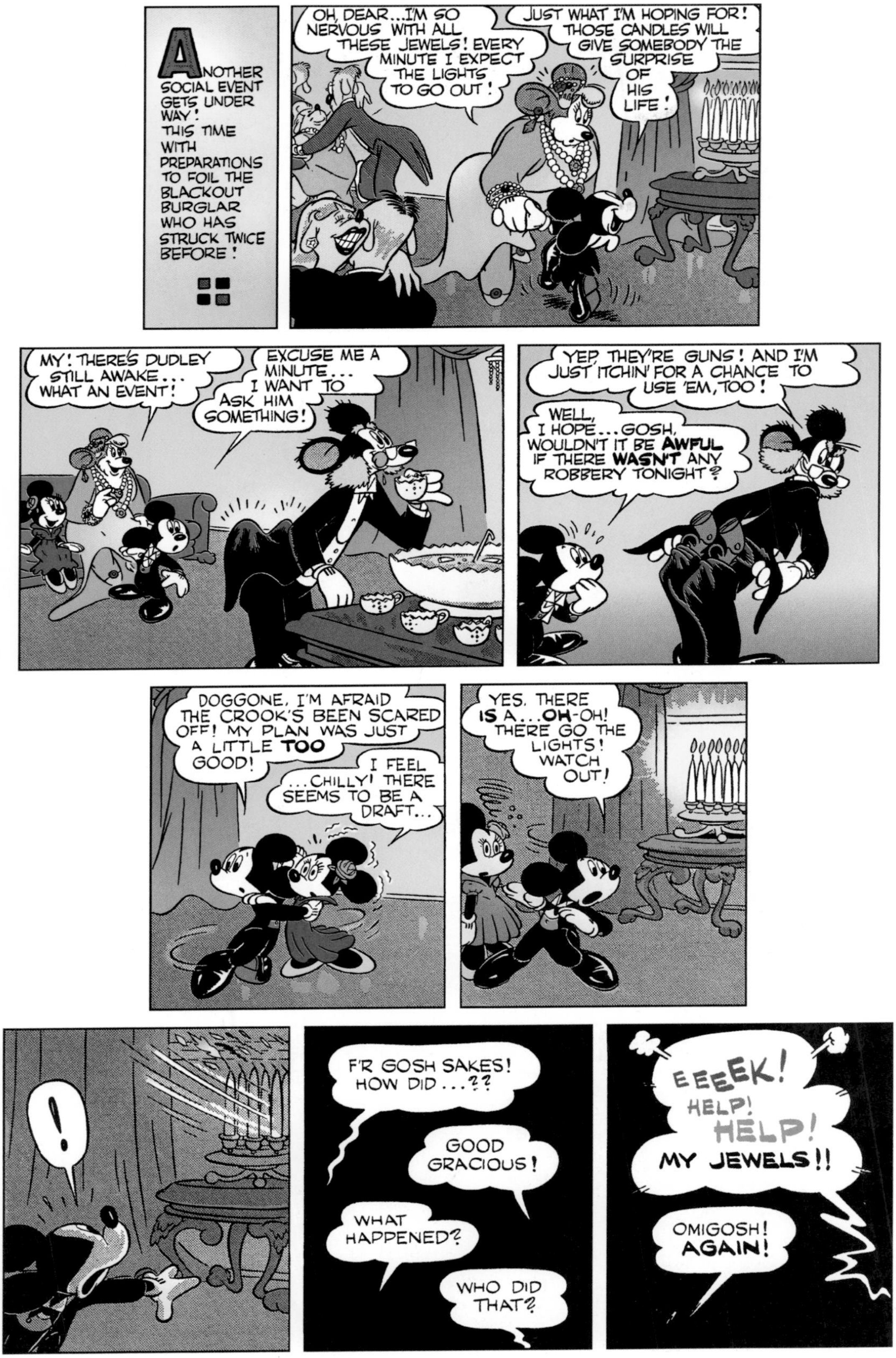
ANOTHER SOCIAL EVENT GETS UNDER WAY! THIS TIME WITH PREPARATIONS TO FOIL THE BLACKOUT BURGLAR WHO HAS STRUCK TWICE BEFORE!
OH, DEAR...I'M SO NERVOUS WITH ALL THESE JEWELS! EVERY MINUTE I EXPECT THE LIGHTS TO GO OUT!
JUST WHAT I'M HOPING FOR! THOSE CANDLES WILL GIVE SOMEBODY THE SURPRISE OF HIS LIFE!
MY! THERE'S DUDLEY STILL AWAKE... WHAT AN EVENT!
EXCUSE ME A MINUTE... I WANT TO ASK HIM SOMETHING!
YEP, THEY'RE GUNS! AND I'M JUST ITCHIN' FOR A CHANCE TO USE 'EM, TOO!
WELL, I HOPE...GOSH, WOULDN'T IT BE **AWFUL** IF THERE **WASN'T** ANY ROBBERY TONIGHT?
DOGGONE, I'M AFRAID THE CROOK'S BEEN SCARED OFF! MY PLAN WAS JUST A LITTLE **TOO** GOOD!
I FEEL ...CHILLY! THERE SEEMS TO BE A DRAFT...
YES, THERE **IS** A...**OH**-OH! THERE GO THE LIGHTS! WATCH OUT!
!
F'R GOSH SAKES! HOW DID...??
GOOD GRACIOUS!
WHAT HAPPENED?
WHO DID THAT?
EEEEK! HELP! HELP! MY JEWELS!!
OMIGOSH! **AGAIN**!

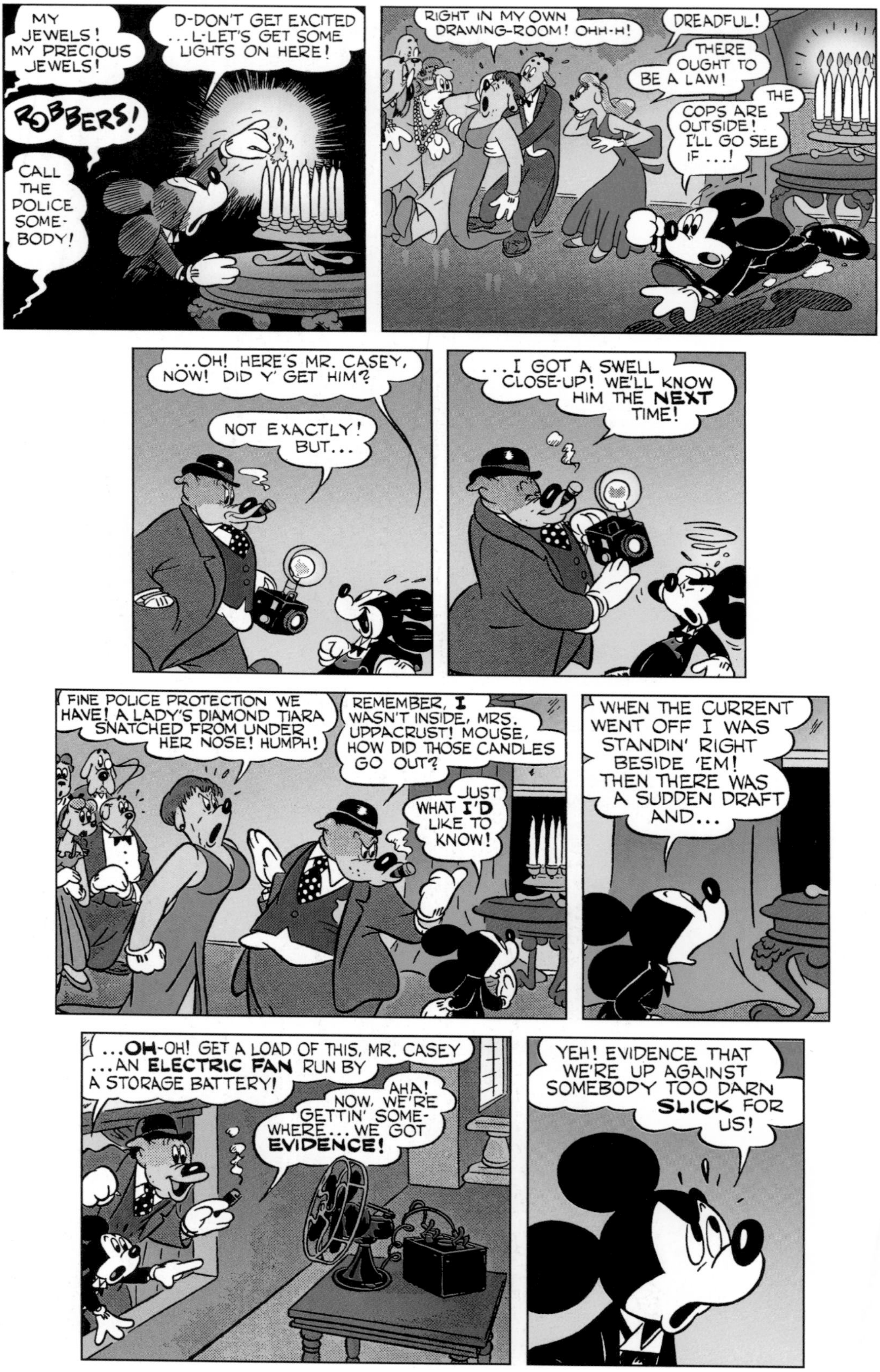

MY JEWELS! MY PRECIOUS JEWELS!
D-DON'T GET EXCITED ... L-LET'S GET SOME LIGHTS ON HERE!
ROBBERS!
CALL THE POLICE SOME-BODY!
RIGHT IN MY OWN DRAWING-ROOM! OHH-H!
DREADFUL!
THERE OUGHT TO BE A LAW!
THE COPS ARE OUTSIDE! I'LL GO SEE IF ...!
...OH! HERE'S MR. CASEY, NOW! DID Y' GET HIM?
NOT EXACTLY! BUT...
...I GOT A SWELL CLOSE-UP! WE'LL KNOW HIM THE NEXT TIME!
FINE POLICE PROTECTION WE HAVE! A LADY'S DIAMOND TIARA SNATCHED FROM UNDER HER NOSE! HUMPH!
REMEMBER, I WASN'T INSIDE, MRS. UPPACRUST! MOUSE, HOW DID THOSE CANDLES GO OUT?
JUST WHAT I'D LIKE TO KNOW!
WHEN THE CURRENT WENT OFF I WAS STANDIN' RIGHT BESIDE 'EM! THEN THERE WAS A SUDDEN DRAFT AND...
...OH-OH! GET A LOAD OF THIS, MR. CASEY ...AN ELECTRIC FAN RUN BY A STORAGE BATTERY!
AHA! NOW, WE'RE GETTIN' SOME-WHERE... WE GOT EVIDENCE!
YEH! EVIDENCE THAT WE'RE UP AGAINST SOMEBODY TOO DARN SLICK FOR US!

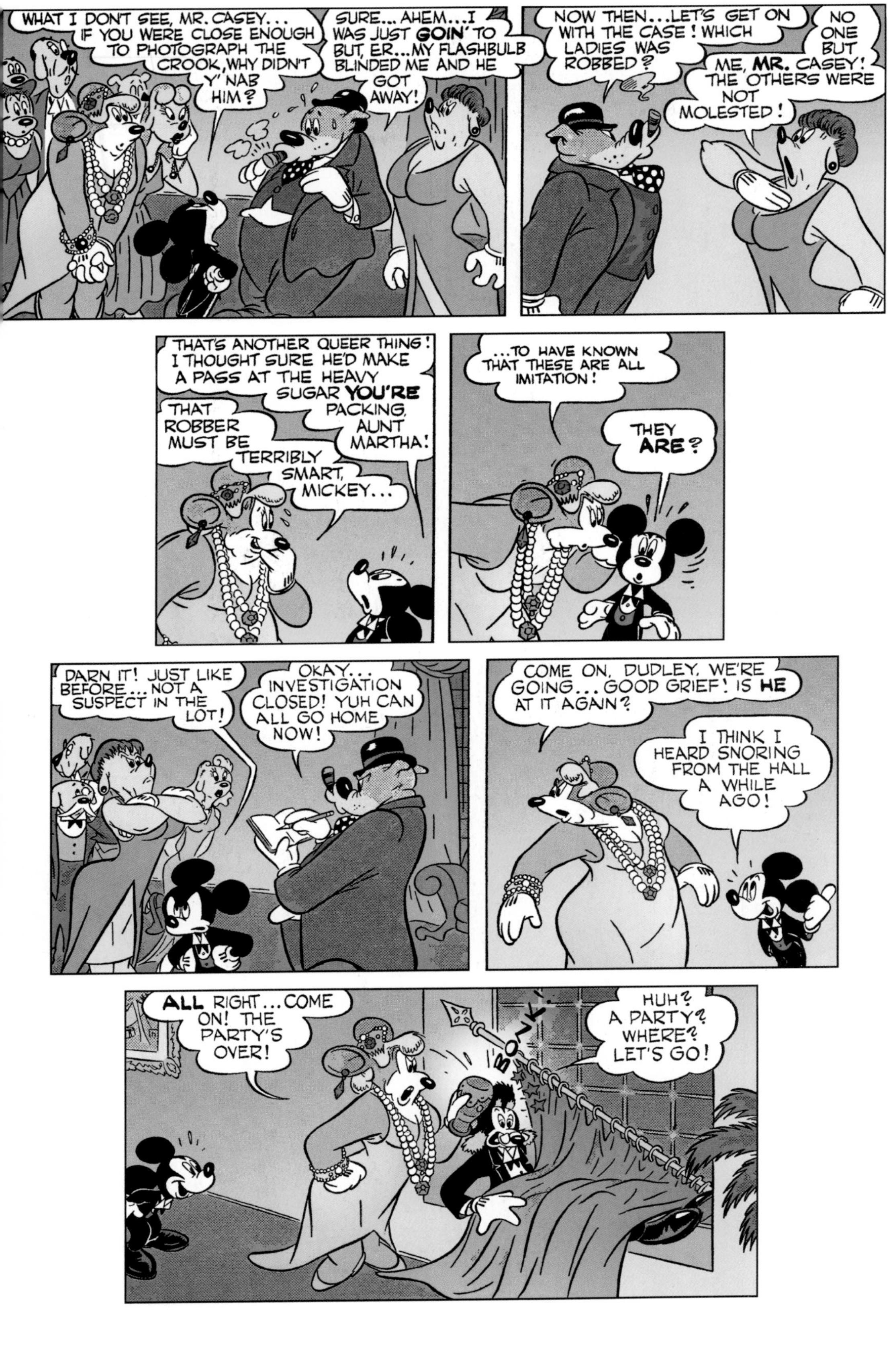
WHAT I DON'T SEE, MR. CASEY... IF YOU WERE CLOSE ENOUGH TO PHOTOGRAPH THE CROOK, WHY DIDN'T Y' NAB HIM?
SURE... AHEM... I WAS JUST GOIN' TO BUT, ER... MY FLASHBULB BLINDED ME AND HE GOT AWAY!
NOW THEN... LET'S GET ON WITH THE CASE! WHICH LADIES WAS ROBBED?
NO ONE BUT ME, MR. CASEY! THE OTHERS WERE NOT MOLESTED!
THAT'S ANOTHER QUEER THING! I THOUGHT SURE HE'D MAKE A PASS AT THE HEAVY SUGAR YOU'RE PACKING, AUNT MARTHA!
THAT ROBBER MUST BE TERRIBLY SMART, MICKEY...
...TO HAVE KNOWN THAT THESE ARE ALL IMITATION!
THEY ARE?
DARN IT! JUST LIKE BEFORE... NOT A SUSPECT IN THE LOT!
OKAY... INVESTIGATION CLOSED! YUH CAN ALL GO HOME NOW!
COME ON, DUDLEY, WE'RE GOING... GOOD GRIEF! IS HE AT IT AGAIN?
I THINK I HEARD SNORING FROM THE HALL A WHILE AGO!
ALL RIGHT... COME ON! THE PARTY'S OVER!
BONK!
HUH? A PARTY? WHERE? LET'S GO!

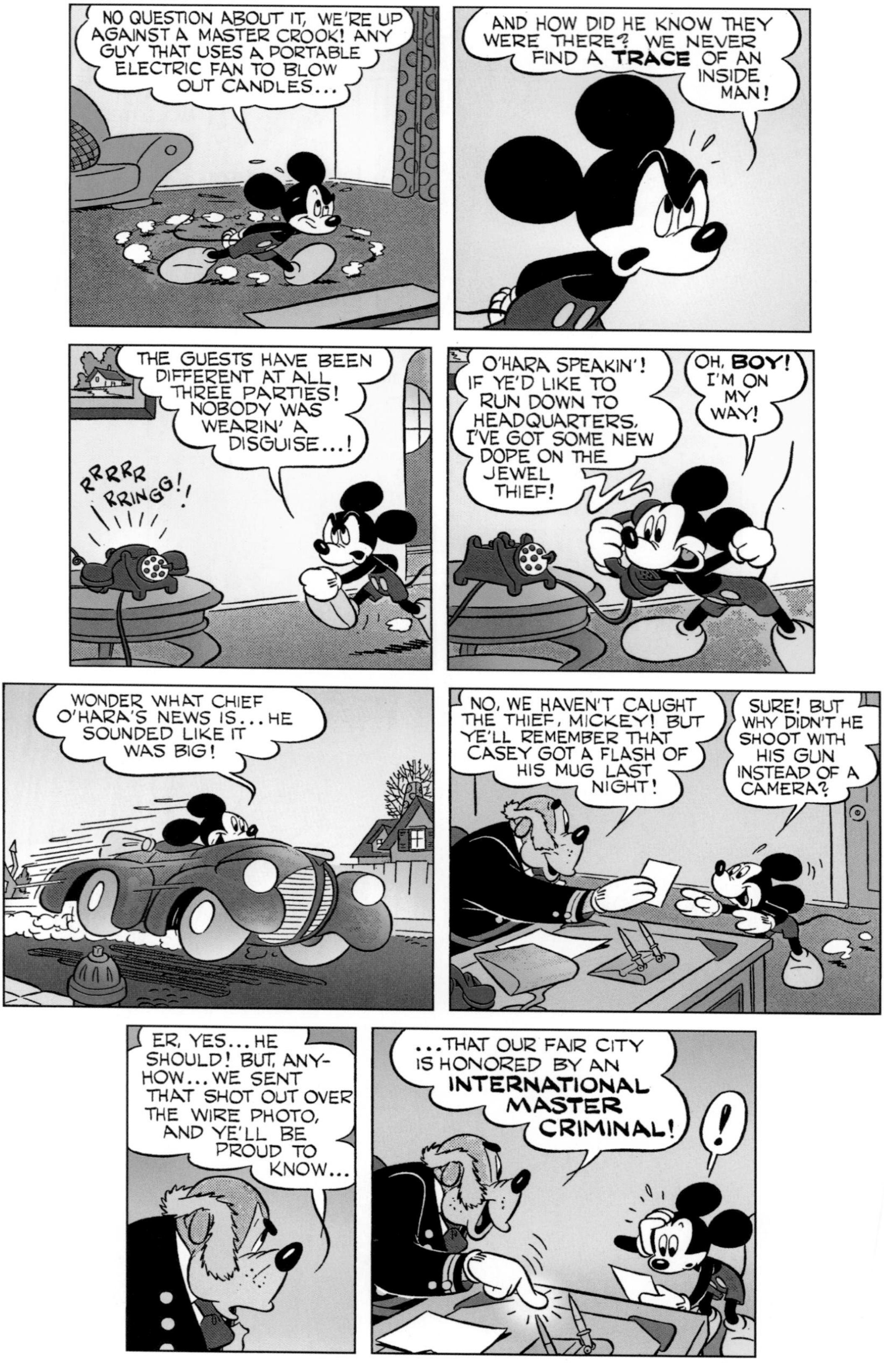
NO QUESTION ABOUT IT, WE'RE UP AGAINST A MASTER CROOK! ANY GUY THAT USES A PORTABLE ELECTRIC FAN TO BLOW OUT CANDLES...
AND HOW DID HE KNOW THEY WERE THERE? WE NEVER FIND A TRACE OF AN INSIDE MAN!
THE GUESTS HAVE BEEN DIFFERENT AT ALL THREE PARTIES! NOBODY WAS WEARIN' A DISGUISE...!
RRRRR RRINGG!!
O'HARA SPEAKIN'! IF YE'D LIKE TO RUN DOWN TO HEADQUARTERS, I'VE GOT SOME NEW DOPE ON THE JEWEL THIEF!
OH, BOY! I'M ON MY WAY!
WONDER WHAT CHIEF O'HARA'S NEWS IS... HE SOUNDED LIKE IT WAS BIG!
NO, WE HAVEN'T CAUGHT THE THIEF, MICKEY! BUT YE'LL REMEMBER THAT CASEY GOT A FLASH OF HIS MUG LAST NIGHT!
SURE! BUT WHY DIDN'T HE SHOOT WITH HIS GUN INSTEAD OF A CAMERA?
ER, YES... HE SHOULD! BUT, ANY-HOW... WE SENT THAT SHOT OUT OVER THE WIRE PHOTO, AND YE'LL BE PROUD TO KNOW...
...THAT OUR FAIR CITY IS HONORED BY AN INTERNATIONAL MASTER CRIMINAL!
!

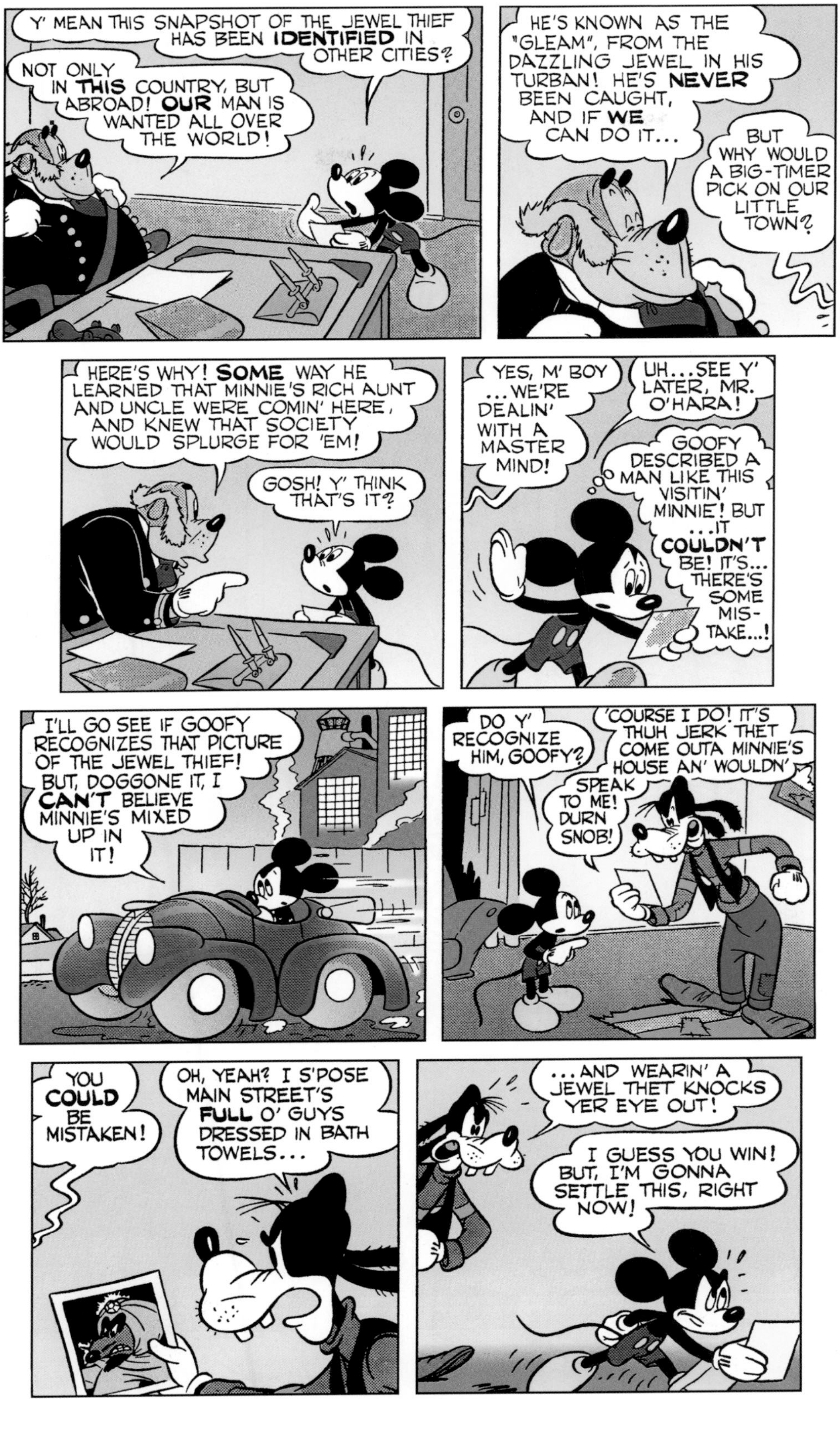
Y' MEAN THIS SNAPSHOT OF THE JEWEL THIEF HAS BEEN **IDENTIFIED** IN OTHER CITIES?
NOT ONLY IN **THIS** COUNTRY, BUT ABROAD! **OUR** MAN IS WANTED ALL OVER THE WORLD!
HE'S KNOWN AS THE "GLEAM", FROM THE DAZZLING JEWEL IN HIS TURBAN! HE'S **NEVER** BEEN CAUGHT, AND IF **WE** CAN DO IT...
BUT WHY WOULD A BIG-TIMER PICK ON OUR LITTLE TOWN?
HERE'S WHY! **SOME** WAY HE LEARNED THAT MINNIE'S RICH AUNT AND UNCLE WERE COMIN' HERE, AND KNEW THAT SOCIETY WOULD SPLURGE FOR 'EM!
GOSH! Y' THINK THAT'S IT?
YES, M' BOY ...WE'RE DEALIN' WITH A MASTER MIND!
UH...SEE Y' LATER, MR. O'HARA!
GOOFY DESCRIBED A MAN LIKE THIS VISITIN' MINNIE! BUT ...IT **COULDN'T** BE! IT'S... THERE'S SOME MIS-TAKE...!
I'LL GO SEE IF GOOFY RECOGNIZES THAT PICTURE OF THE JEWEL THIEF! BUT, DOGGONE IT, I **CAN'T** BELIEVE MINNIE'S MIXED UP IN IT!
DO Y' RECOGNIZE HIM, GOOFY?
'COURSE I DO! IT'S THUH JERK THET COME OUTA MINNIE'S HOUSE AN' WOULDN' SPEAK TO ME! DURN SNOB!
YOU **COULD** BE MISTAKEN!
OH, YEAH? I S'POSE MAIN STREET'S **FULL** O' GUYS DRESSED IN BATH TOWELS...
...AND WEARIN' A JEWEL THET KNOCKS YER EYE OUT!
I GUESS YOU WIN! BUT, I'M GONNA SETTLE THIS, RIGHT NOW!

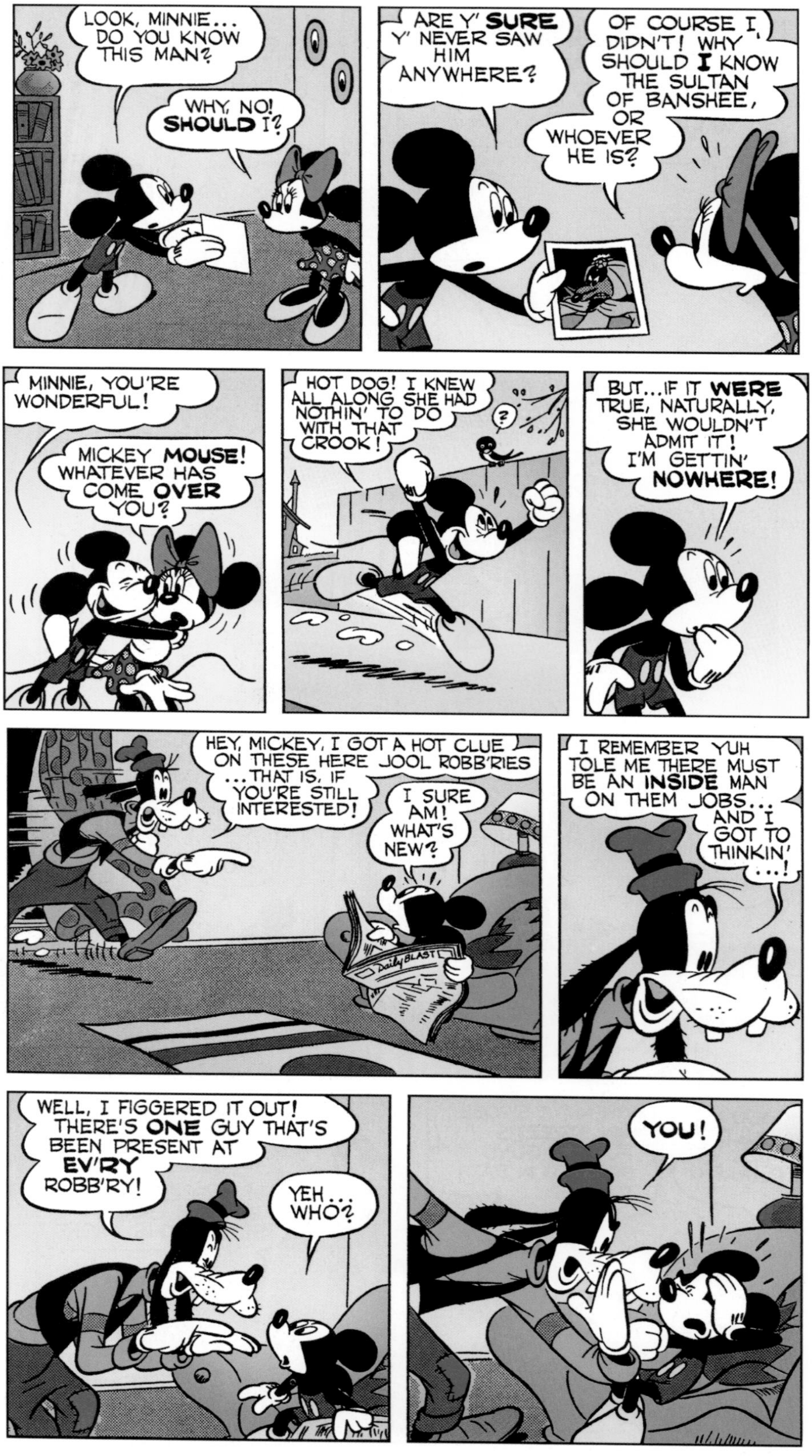
LOOK, MINNIE... DO YOU KNOW THIS MAN?
WHY, NO! SHOULD I?
ARE Y' SURE Y' NEVER SAW HIM ANYWHERE?
OF COURSE I DIDN'T! WHY SHOULD I KNOW THE SULTAN OF BANSHEE, OR WHOEVER HE IS?
MINNIE, YOU'RE WONDERFUL!
MICKEY MOUSE! WHATEVER HAS COME OVER YOU?
HOT DOG! I KNEW ALL ALONG SHE HAD NOTHIN' TO DO WITH THAT CROOK!
?
BUT...IF IT WERE TRUE, NATURALLY, SHE WOULDN'T ADMIT IT! I'M GETTIN' NOWHERE!
HEY, MICKEY, I GOT A HOT CLUE ON THESE HERE JOOL ROBB'RIES ...THAT IS, IF YOU'RE STILL INTERESTED!
I SURE AM! WHAT'S NEW?
Daily BLAST
I REMEMBER YUH TOLE ME THERE MUST BE AN INSIDE MAN ON THEM JOBS... AND I GOT TO THINKIN' ...!
WELL, I FIGGERED IT OUT! THERE'S ONE GUY THAT'S BEEN PRESENT AT EV'RY ROBB'RY!
YEH... WHO?
YOU!

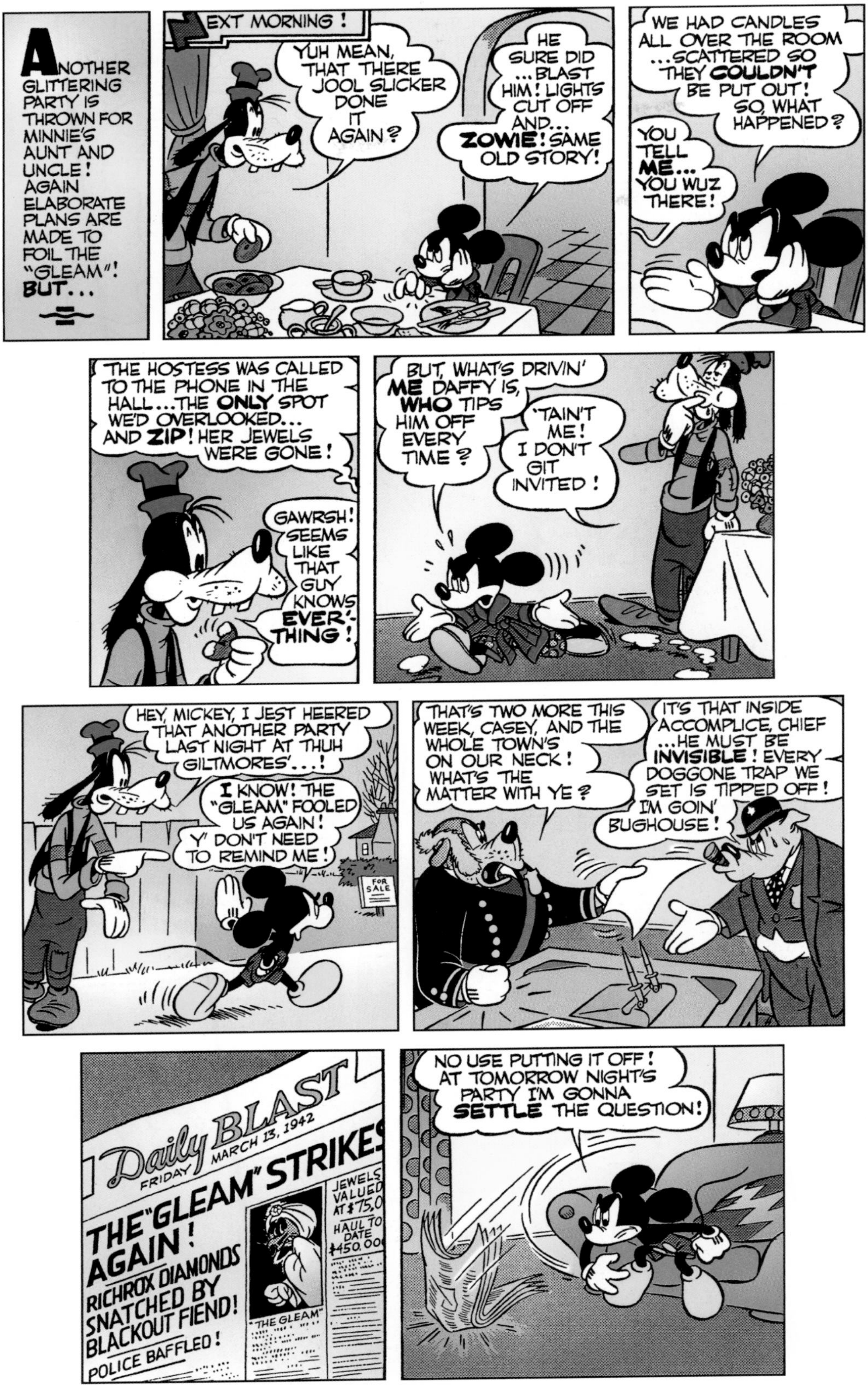

ANOTHER GLITTERING PARTY IS THROWN FOR MINNIE'S AUNT AND UNCLE! AGAIN ELABORATE PLANS ARE MADE TO FOIL THE "GLEAM"! BUT...
NEXT MORNING!
YUH MEAN, THAT THERE JOOL SLICKER DONE IT AGAIN?
HE SURE DID ...BLAST HIM! LIGHTS CUT OFF AND... ZOWIE! SAME OLD STORY!
WE HAD CANDLES ALL OVER THE ROOM ...SCATTERED SO THEY COULDN'T BE PUT OUT! SO, WHAT HAPPENED?
YOU TELL ME... YOU WUZ THERE!
THE HOSTESS WAS CALLED TO THE PHONE IN THE HALL...THE ONLY SPOT WE'D OVERLOOKED... AND ZIP! HER JEWELS WERE GONE!
GAWRSH! SEEMS LIKE THAT GUY KNOWS EVER'-THING!
BUT, WHAT'S DRIVIN' ME DAFFY IS, WHO TIPS HIM OFF EVERY TIME?
'TAIN'T ME! I DON'T GIT INVITED!
HEY, MICKEY, I JEST HEERED THAT ANOTHER PARTY LAST NIGHT AT THUH GILTMORES'...!
I KNOW! THE "GLEAM" FOOLED US AGAIN! Y' DON'T NEED TO REMIND ME!
FOR SALE
THAT'S TWO MORE THIS WEEK, CASEY, AND THE WHOLE TOWN'S ON OUR NECK! WHAT'S THE MATTER WITH YE?
IT'S THAT INSIDE ACCOMPLICE, CHIEF ...HE MUST BE INVISIBLE! EVERY DOGGONE TRAP WE SET IS TIPPED OFF! I'M GOIN' BUGHOUSE!
Daily BLAST
FRIDAY MARCH 13, 1942
"GLEAM" STRIKES
THE "GLEAM" AGAIN!
RICHROX DIAMONDS SNATCHED BY BLACKOUT FIEND!
POLICE BAFFLED!
JEWELS VALUED AT $75,0
HAUL TO DATE $450,00
"THE GLEAM"
NO USE PUTTING IT OFF! AT TOMORROW NIGHT'S PARTY I'M GONNA SETTLE THE QUESTION!

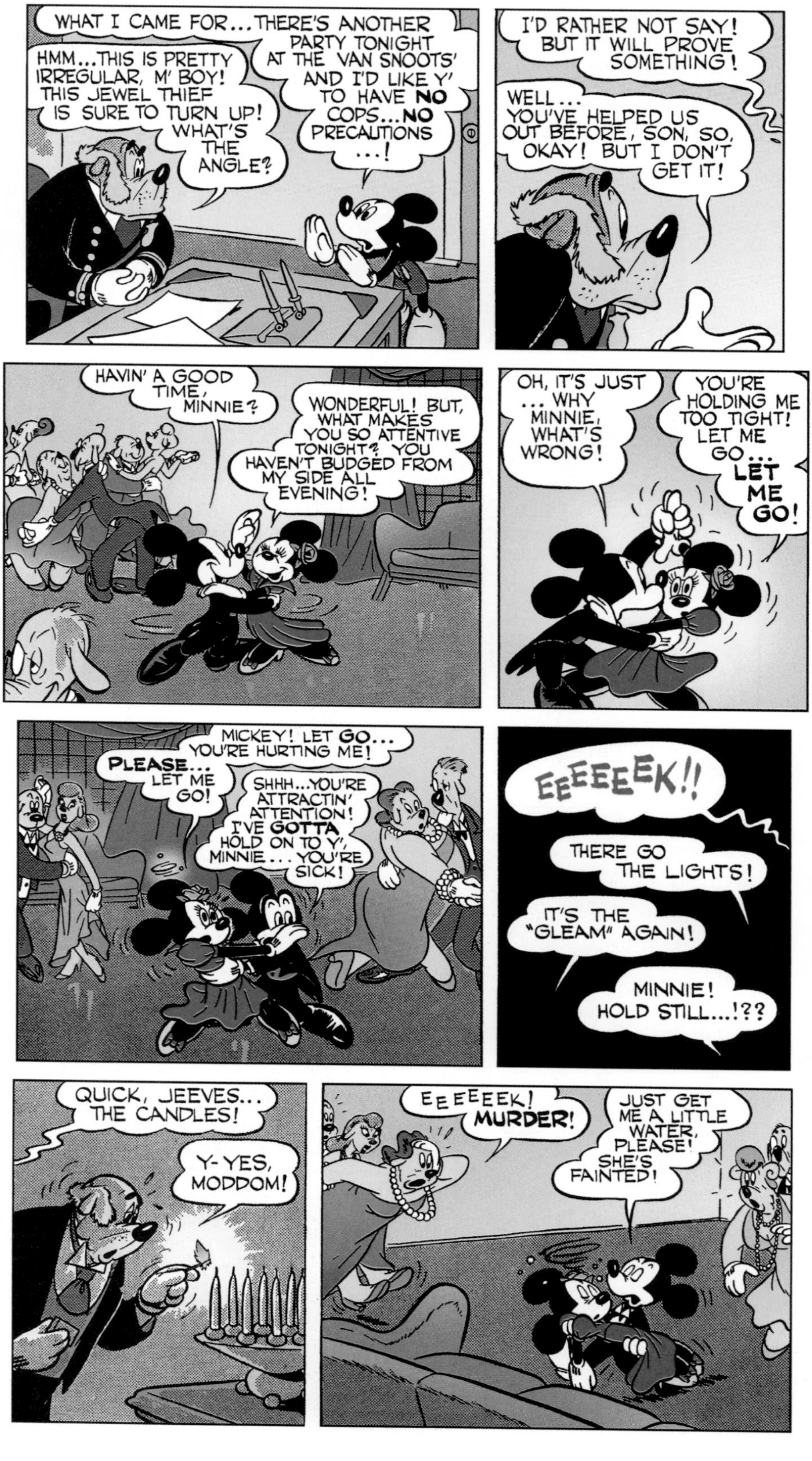

HMM...THIS IS PRETTY IRREGULAR, M' BOY! THIS JEWEL THIEF IS SURE TO TURN UP! WHAT'S THE ANGLE?
WHAT I CAME FOR...THERE'S ANOTHER PARTY TONIGHT AT THE VAN SNOOTS' AND I'D LIKE Y' TO HAVE NO COPS...NO PRECAUTIONS ...!
I'D RATHER NOT SAY! BUT IT WILL PROVE SOMETHING!
WELL... YOU'VE HELPED US OUT BEFORE, SON, SO, OKAY! BUT I DON'T GET IT!
HAVIN' A GOOD TIME, MINNIE?
WONDERFUL! BUT, WHAT MAKES YOU SO ATTENTIVE TONIGHT? YOU HAVEN'T BUDGED FROM MY SIDE ALL EVENING!
YOU'RE HOLDING ME TOO TIGHT! LET ME GO... LET ME GO!
OH, IT'S JUST ... WHY MINNIE, WHAT'S WRONG!
MICKEY! LET GO... YOU'RE HURTING ME!
PLEASE... LET ME GO!
SHHH...YOU'RE ATTRACTIN' ATTENTION! I'VE GOTTA HOLD ON TO Y', MINNIE... YOU'RE SICK!
EEEEEEK!!
THERE GO THE LIGHTS!
IT'S THE "GLEAM" AGAIN!
MINNIE! HOLD STILL...!??
QUICK, JEEVES... THE CANDLES!
Y-YES, MODDOM!
EEEEEEK! MURDER!
JUST GET ME A LITTLE WATER, PLEASE! SHE'S FAINTED!

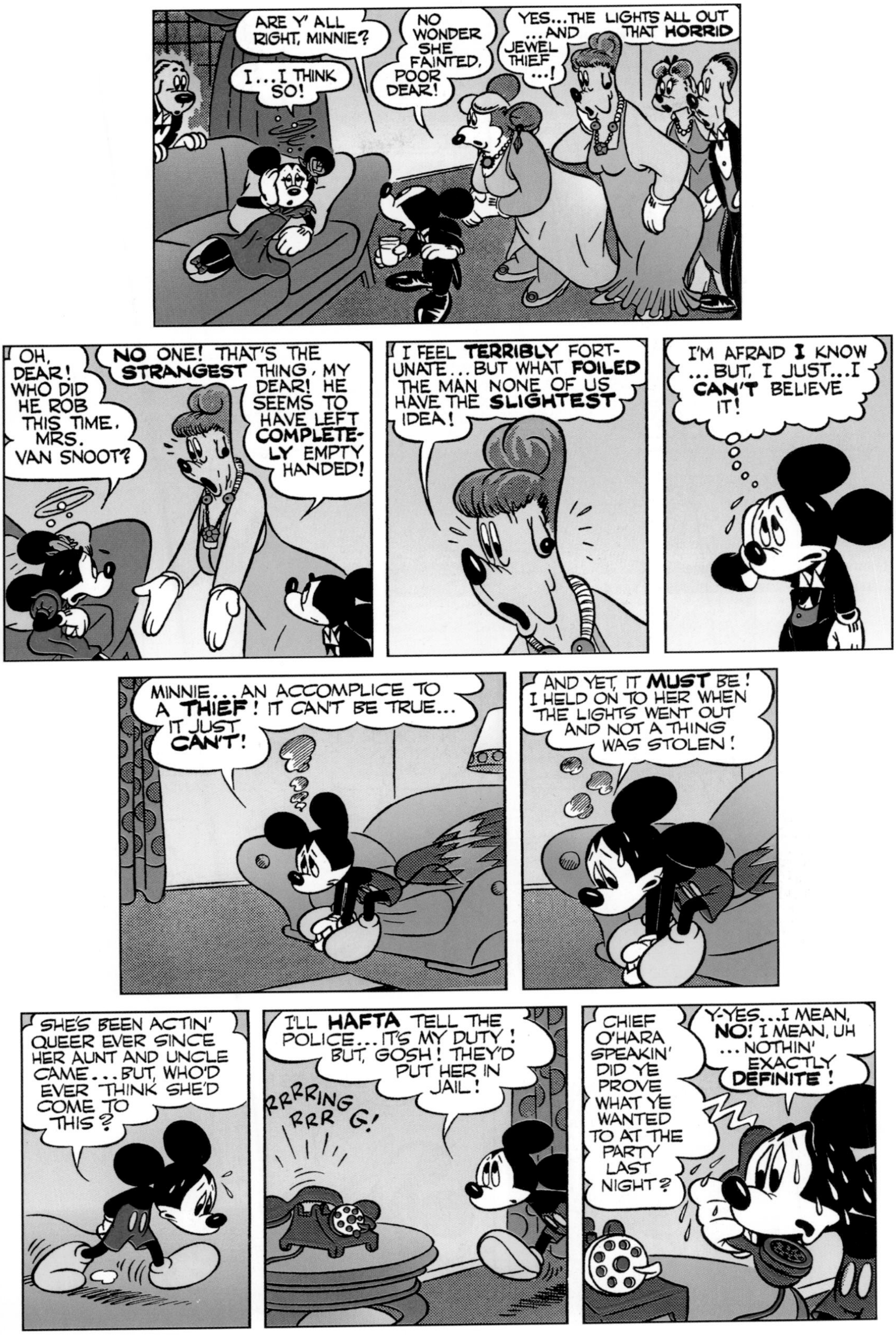
ARE Y' ALL RIGHT, MINNIE?
I...I THINK SO!
NO WONDER SHE FAINTED, POOR DEAR!
YES...THE LIGHTS ALL OUT ...AND THAT HORRID JEWEL THIEF ...!
OH, DEAR! WHO DID HE ROB THIS TIME, MRS. VAN SNOOT?
NO ONE! THAT'S THE STRANGEST THING, MY DEAR! HE SEEMS TO HAVE LEFT COMPLETELY EMPTY HANDED!
I FEEL TERRIBLY FORTUNATE... BUT WHAT FOILED THE MAN NONE OF US HAVE THE SLIGHTEST IDEA!
I'M AFRAID I KNOW ... BUT, I JUST...I CAN'T BELIEVE IT!
MINNIE...AN ACCOMPLICE TO A THIEF! IT CAN'T BE TRUE... IT JUST CAN'T!
AND YET, IT MUST BE! I HELD ON TO HER WHEN THE LIGHTS WENT OUT AND NOT A THING WAS STOLEN!
SHE'S BEEN ACTIN' QUEER EVER SINCE HER AUNT AND UNCLE CAME...BUT, WHO'D EVER THINK SHE'D COME TO THIS?
I'LL HAFTA TELL THE POLICE...IT'S MY DUTY! BUT, GOSH! THEY'D PUT HER IN JAIL!
RRRRING RRR G!
CHIEF O'HARA SPEAKIN' DID YE PROVE WHAT YE WANTED TO AT THE PARTY LAST NIGHT?
Y-YES...I MEAN, NO! I MEAN, UH ... NOTHIN' EXACTLY DEFINITE!

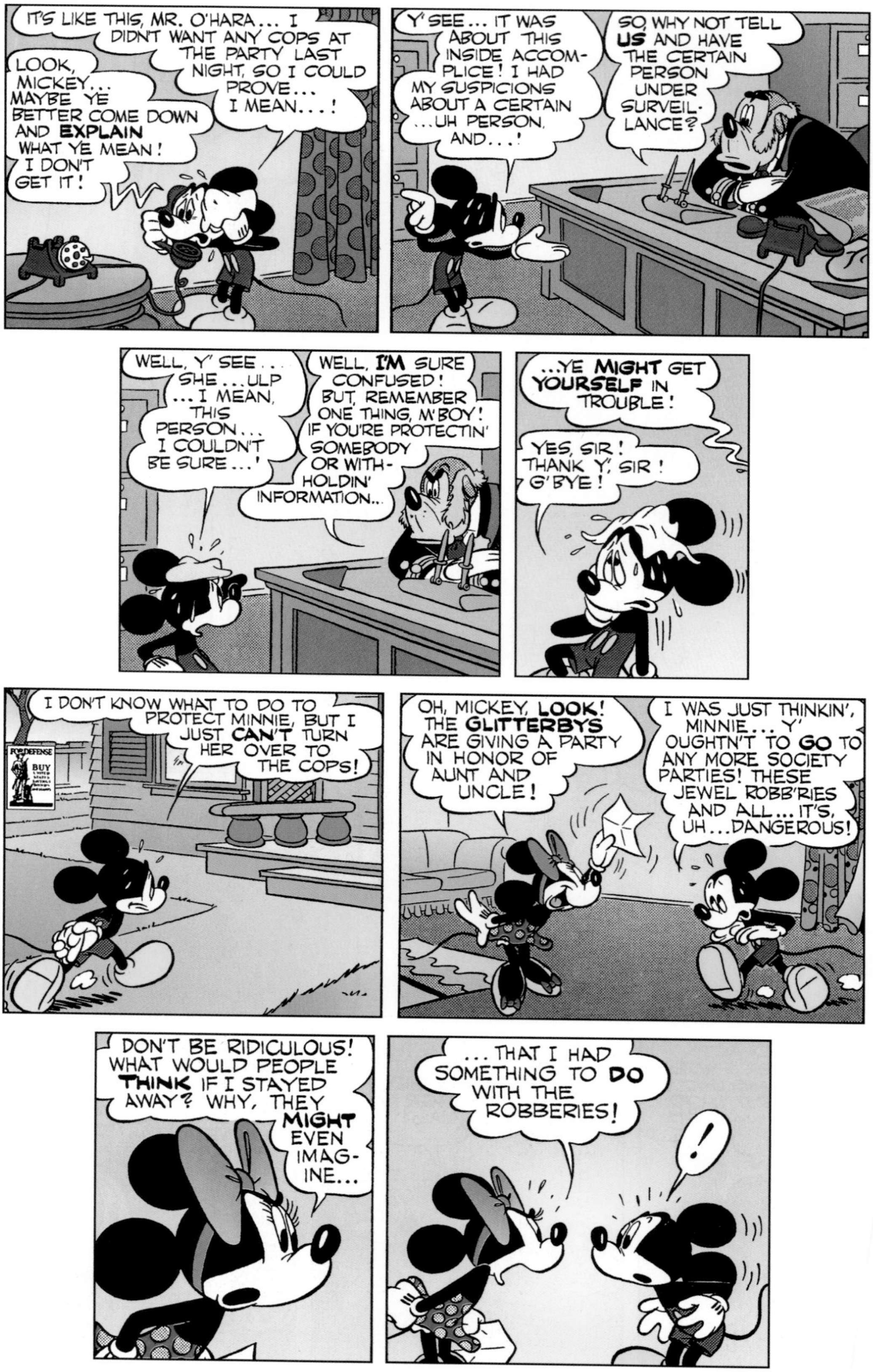

IT'S LIKE THIS, MR. O'HARA... I DIDN'T WANT ANY COPS AT THE PARTY LAST NIGHT, SO I COULD PROVE... I MEAN...!
LOOK, MICKEY... MAYBE YE BETTER COME DOWN AND EXPLAIN WHAT YE MEAN! I DON'T GET IT!
Y' SEE... IT WAS ABOUT THIS INSIDE ACCOMPLICE! I HAD MY SUSPICIONS ABOUT A CERTAIN ...UH PERSON, AND...!
SO, WHY NOT TELL US AND HAVE THE CERTAIN PERSON UNDER SURVEILLANCE?
WELL, Y' SEE... SHE...ULP ...I MEAN, THIS PERSON... I COULDN'T BE SURE...!
WELL, I'M SURE CONFUSED! BUT, REMEMBER ONE THING, M'BOY! IF YOU'RE PROTECTIN' SOMEBODY OR WITHHOLDIN' INFORMATION...
...YE MIGHT GET YOURSELF IN TROUBLE!
YES, SIR! THANK Y', SIR! G'BYE!
I DON'T KNOW WHAT TO DO TO PROTECT MINNIE, BUT I JUST CAN'T TURN HER OVER TO THE COPS!
FOR DEFENSE
BUY
OH, MICKEY, LOOK! THE GLITTERBYS ARE GIVING A PARTY IN HONOR OF AUNT AND UNCLE!
I WAS JUST THINKIN', MINNIE... Y' OUGHTN'T TO GO TO ANY MORE SOCIETY PARTIES! THESE JEWEL ROBB'RIES AND ALL... IT'S, UH...DANGEROUS!
DON'T BE RIDICULOUS! WHAT WOULD PEOPLE THINK IF I STAYED AWAY? WHY, THEY MIGHT EVEN IMAGINE...
...THAT I HAD SOMETHING TO DO WITH THE ROBBERIES!
!

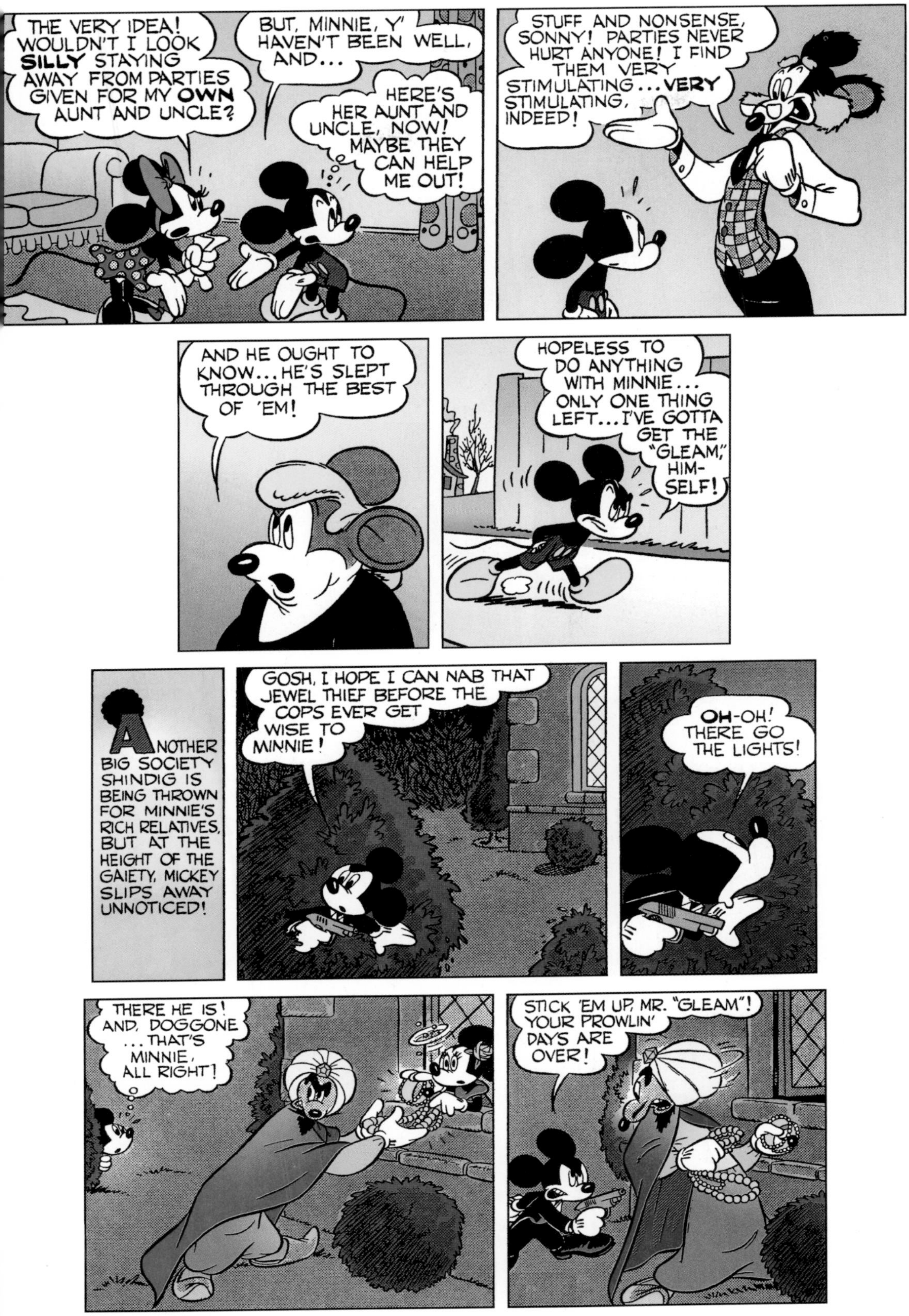
THE VERY IDEA! WOULDN'T I LOOK SILLY STAYING AWAY FROM PARTIES GIVEN FOR MY OWN AUNT AND UNCLE?
BUT, MINNIE, Y' HAVEN'T BEEN WELL, AND...
HERE'S HER AUNT AND UNCLE, NOW! MAYBE THEY CAN HELP ME OUT!
STUFF AND NONSENSE, SONNY! PARTIES NEVER HURT ANYONE! I FIND THEM VERY STIMULATING... VERY STIMULATING, INDEED!
AND HE OUGHT TO KNOW... HE'S SLEPT THROUGH THE BEST OF 'EM!
HOPELESS TO DO ANYTHING WITH MINNIE... ONLY ONE THING LEFT... I'VE GOTTA GET THE "GLEAM," HIM-SELF!
ANOTHER BIG SOCIETY SHINDIG IS BEING THROWN FOR MINNIE'S RICH RELATIVES, BUT AT THE HEIGHT OF THE GAIETY, MICKEY SLIPS AWAY UNNOTICED!
GOSH, I HOPE I CAN NAB THAT JEWEL THIEF BEFORE THE COPS EVER GET WISE TO MINNIE!
OH-OH! THERE GO THE LIGHTS!
THERE HE IS! AND, DOGGONE ... THAT'S MINNIE, ALL RIGHT!
STICK 'EM UP, MR. "GLEAM"! YOUR PROWLIN' DAYS ARE OVER!

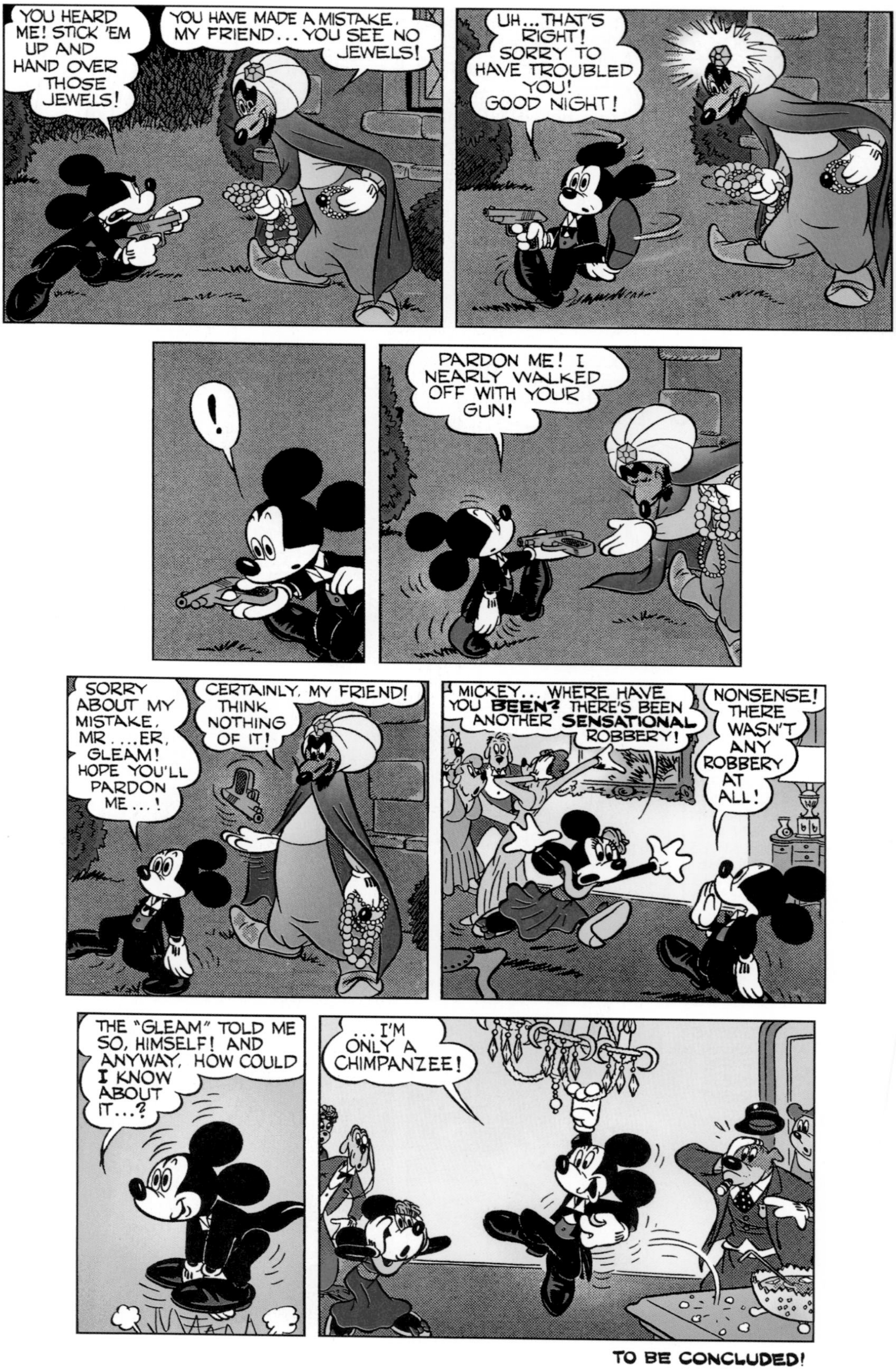
YOU HEARD ME! STICK 'EM UP AND HAND OVER THOSE JEWELS!
YOU HAVE MADE A MISTAKE, MY FRIEND... YOU SEE NO JEWELS!
UH... THAT'S RIGHT! SORRY TO HAVE TROUBLED YOU! GOOD NIGHT!
!
PARDON ME! I NEARLY WALKED OFF WITH YOUR GUN!
SORRY ABOUT MY MISTAKE, MR....ER, GLEAM! HOPE YOU'LL PARDON ME...!
CERTAINLY, MY FRIEND! THINK NOTHING OF IT!
MICKEY... WHERE HAVE YOU BEEN? THERE'S BEEN ANOTHER SENSATIONAL ROBBERY!
NONSENSE! THERE WASN'T ANY ROBBERY AT ALL!
THE "GLEAM" TOLD ME SO, HIMSELF! AND ANYWAY, HOW COULD I KNOW ABOUT IT...?
... I'M ONLY A CHIMPANZEE!

TO BE CONCLUDED!

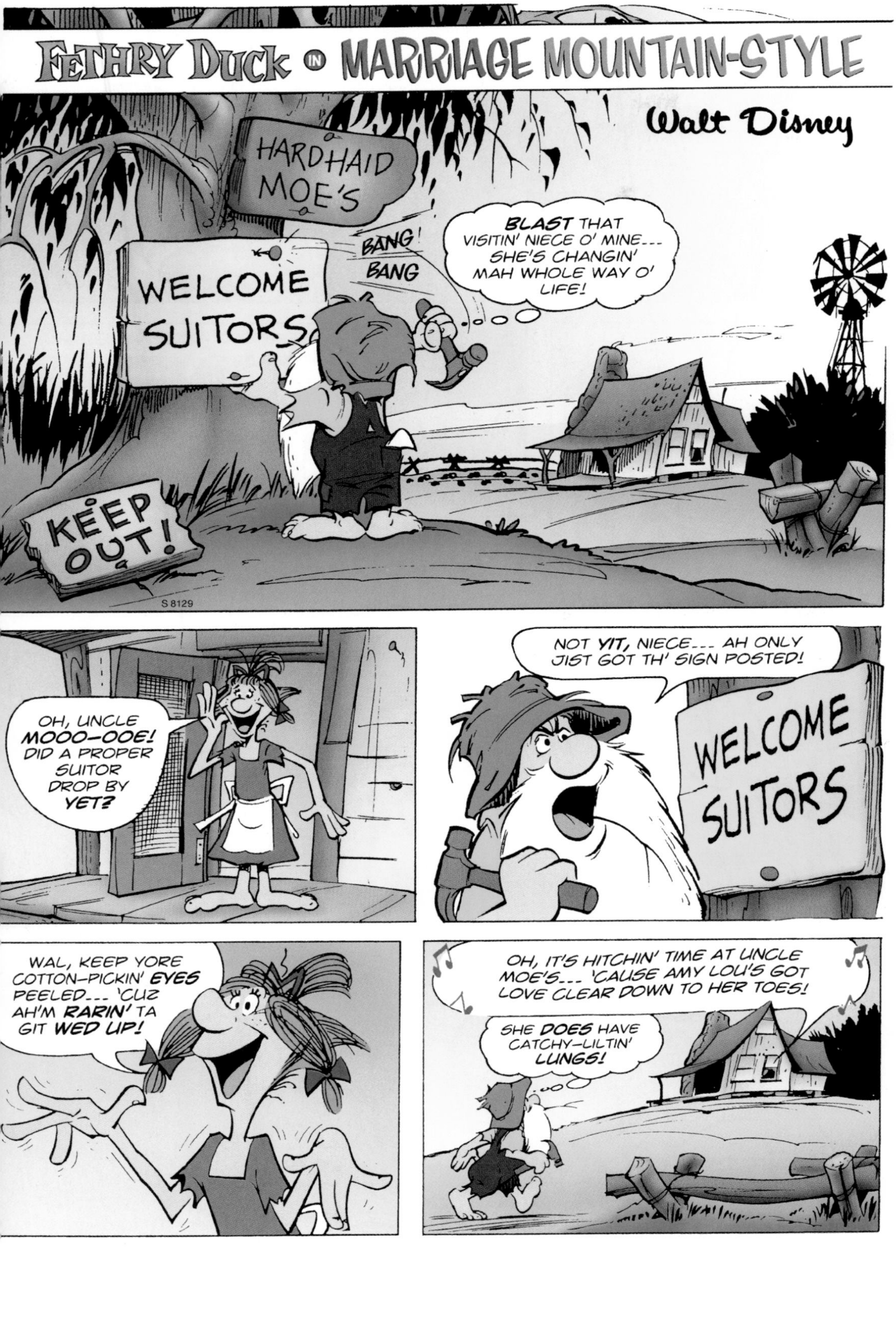
FETHRY DUCK IN MARRIAGE MOUNTAIN-STYLE
Walt Disney
HARDHAID MOE'S
WELCOME SUITORS
KEEP OUT!
BANG BANG
BLAST THAT VISITIN' NIECE O' MINE--- SHE'S CHANGIN' MAH WHOLE WAY O' LIFE!
S 8129
OH, UNCLE MOOO-OOE! DID A PROPER SUITOR DROP BY YET?
NOT YIT, NIECE--- AH ONLY JIST GOT TH' SIGN POSTED!
WELCOME SUITORS
WAL, KEEP YORE COTTON-PICKIN' EYES PEELED--- 'CUZ AH'M RARIN' TA GIT WED UP!
OH, IT'S HITCHIN' TIME AT UNCLE MOE'S--- 'CAUSE AMY LOU'S GOT LOVE CLEAR DOWN TO HER TOES!
SHE DOES HAVE CATCHY-LILTIN' LUNGS!

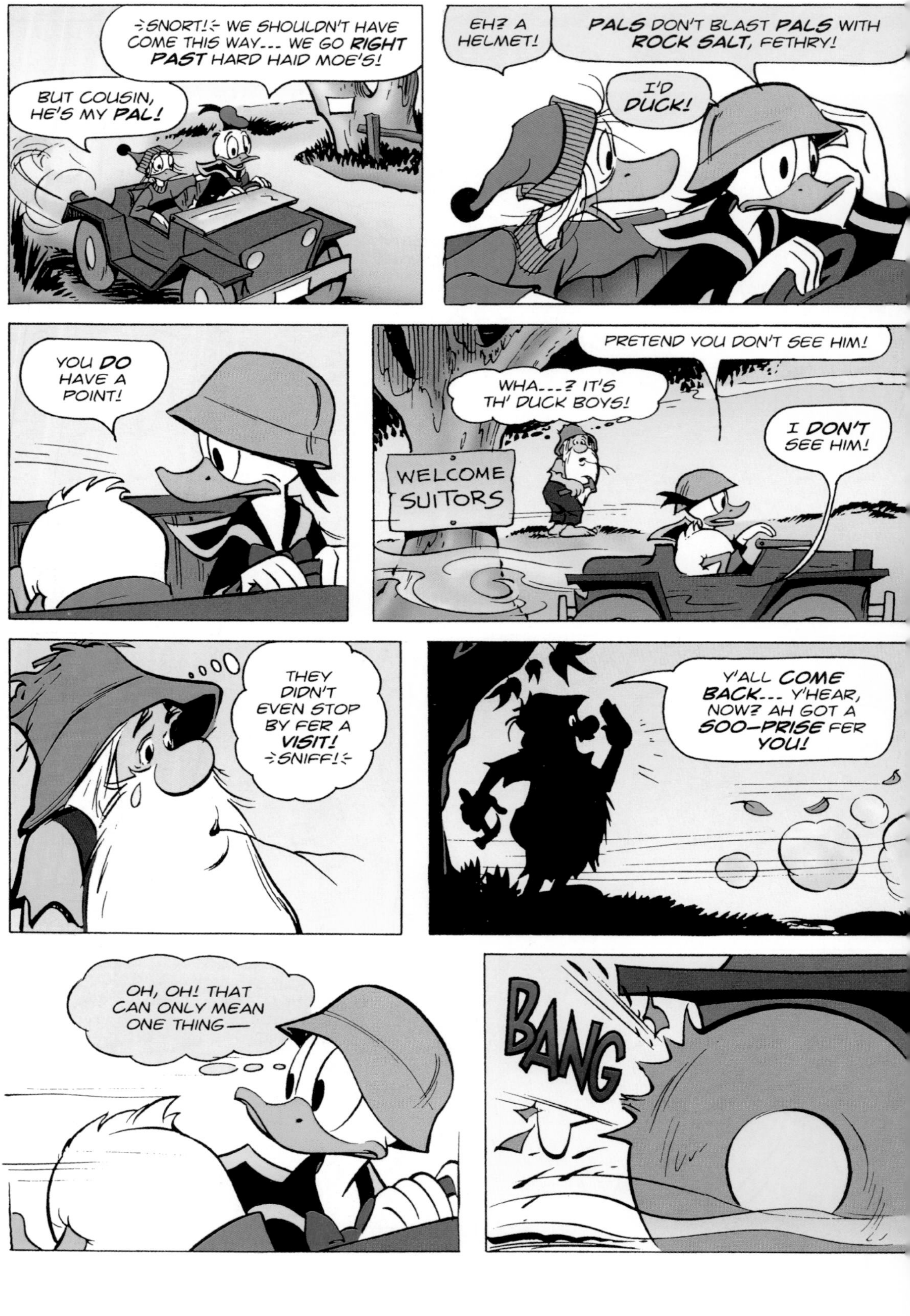

-SNORT!- WE SHOULDN'T HAVE COME THIS WAY--- WE GO RIGHT PAST HARD HAID MOE'S!
BUT COUSIN, HE'S MY PAL!
EH? A HELMET!
PALS DON'T BLAST PALS WITH ROCK SALT, FETHRY!
I'D DUCK!
YOU DO HAVE A POINT!
PRETEND YOU DON'T SEE HIM!
WHA---? IT'S TH' DUCK BOYS!
I DON'T SEE HIM!
WELCOME SUITORS
THEY DIDN'T EVEN STOP BY FER A VISIT! -SNIFF!-
Y'ALL COME BACK--- Y'HEAR, NOW? AH GOT A SOO-PRISE FER YOU!
OH, OH! THAT CAN ONLY MEAN ONE THING—
BANG

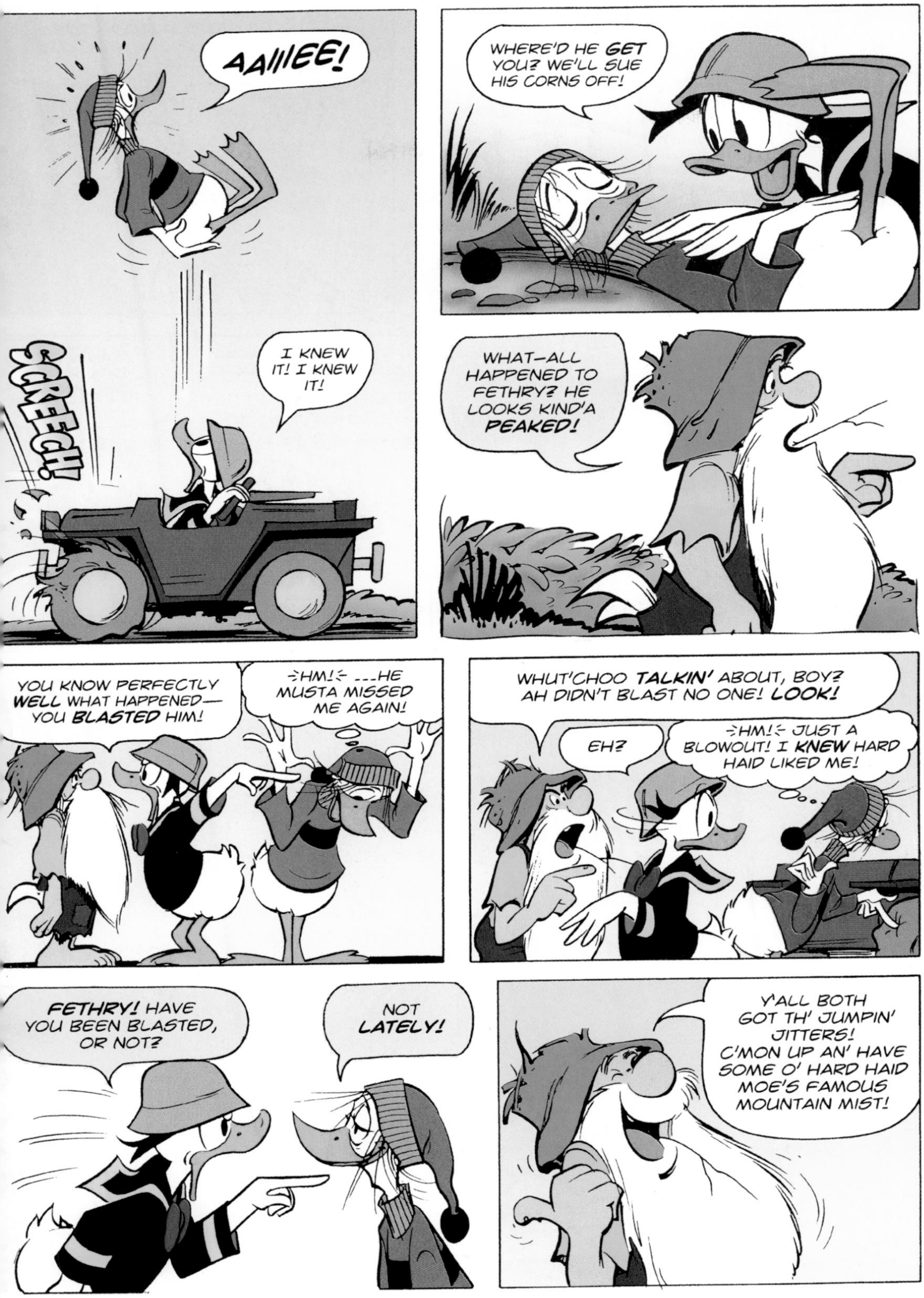

AAIIIEE!
SCREECH!
I KNEW IT! I KNEW IT!
WHERE'D HE **GET** YOU? WE'LL SUE HIS CORNS OFF!
WHAT—ALL HAPPENED TO FETHRY? HE LOOKS KIND'A **PEAKED!**
YOU KNOW PERFECTLY **WELL** WHAT HAPPENED— YOU **BLASTED** HIM!
=HM!= ---HE MUSTA MISSED ME AGAIN!
WHUT'CHOO **TALKIN'** ABOUT, BOY? AH DIDN'T BLAST NO ONE! **LOOK!**
EH?
=HM!= JUST A BLOWOUT! I **KNEW** HARD HAID LIKED ME!
FETHRY! HAVE YOU BEEN BLASTED, OR NOT?
NOT **LATELY!**
Y'ALL BOTH GOT TH' JUMPIN' JITTERS! C'MON UP AN' HAVE SOME O' HARD HAID MOE'S FAMOUS MOUNTAIN MIST!

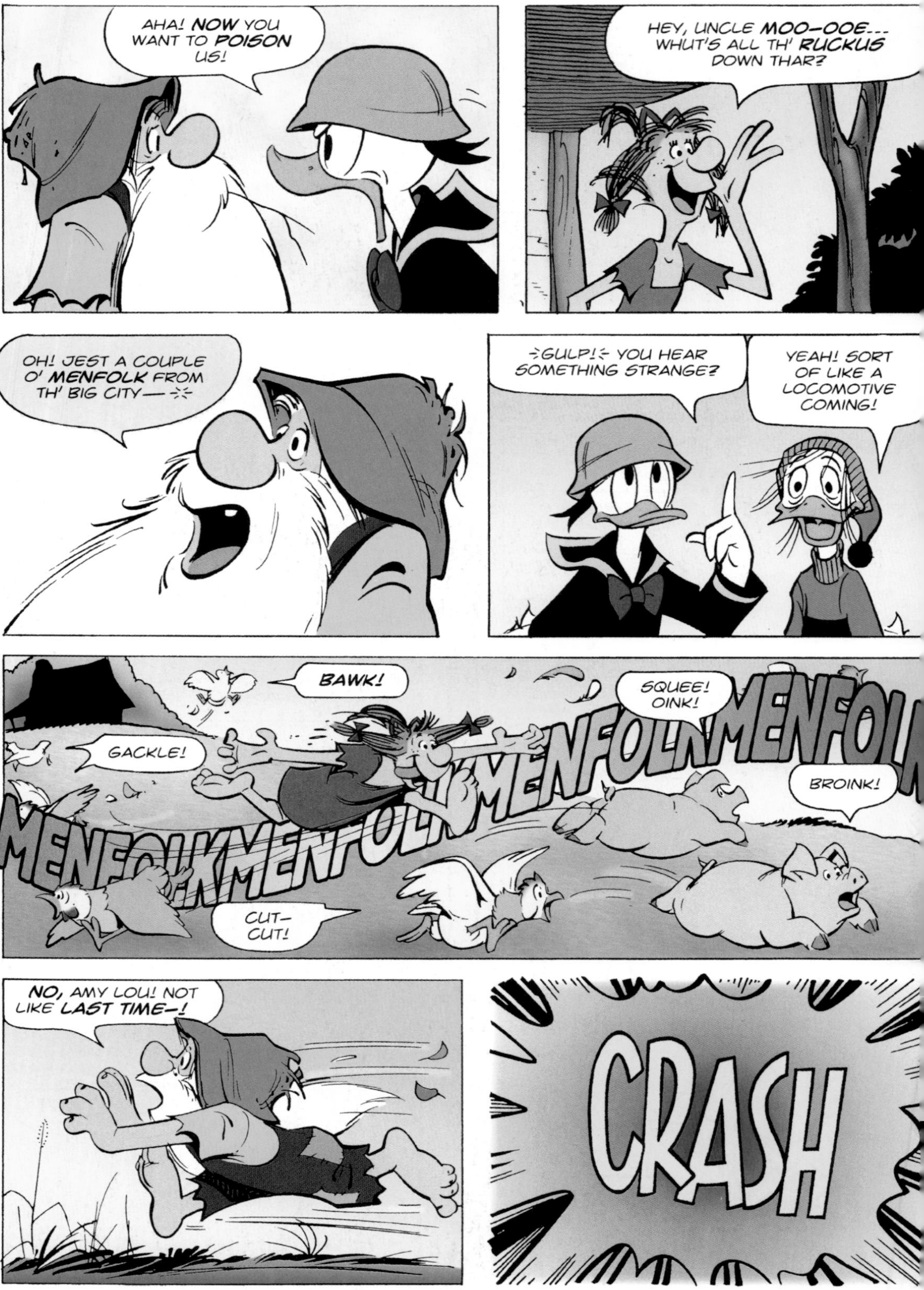
AHA! NOW YOU WANT TO POISON US!
HEY, UNCLE MOO-OOE... WHUT'S ALL TH' RUCKUS DOWN THAR?
OH! JEST A COUPLE O' MENFOLK FROM TH' BIG CITY—
GULP! YOU HEAR SOMETHING STRANGE?
YEAH! SORT OF LIKE A LOCOMOTIVE COMING!
BAWK!
SQUEE! OINK!
GACKLE!
MENFOLKMENFOLKMENFOLKMENFOLKMENFOLK
BROINK!
CUT-CUT!
NO, AMY LOU! NOT LIKE LAST TIME-!
CRASH

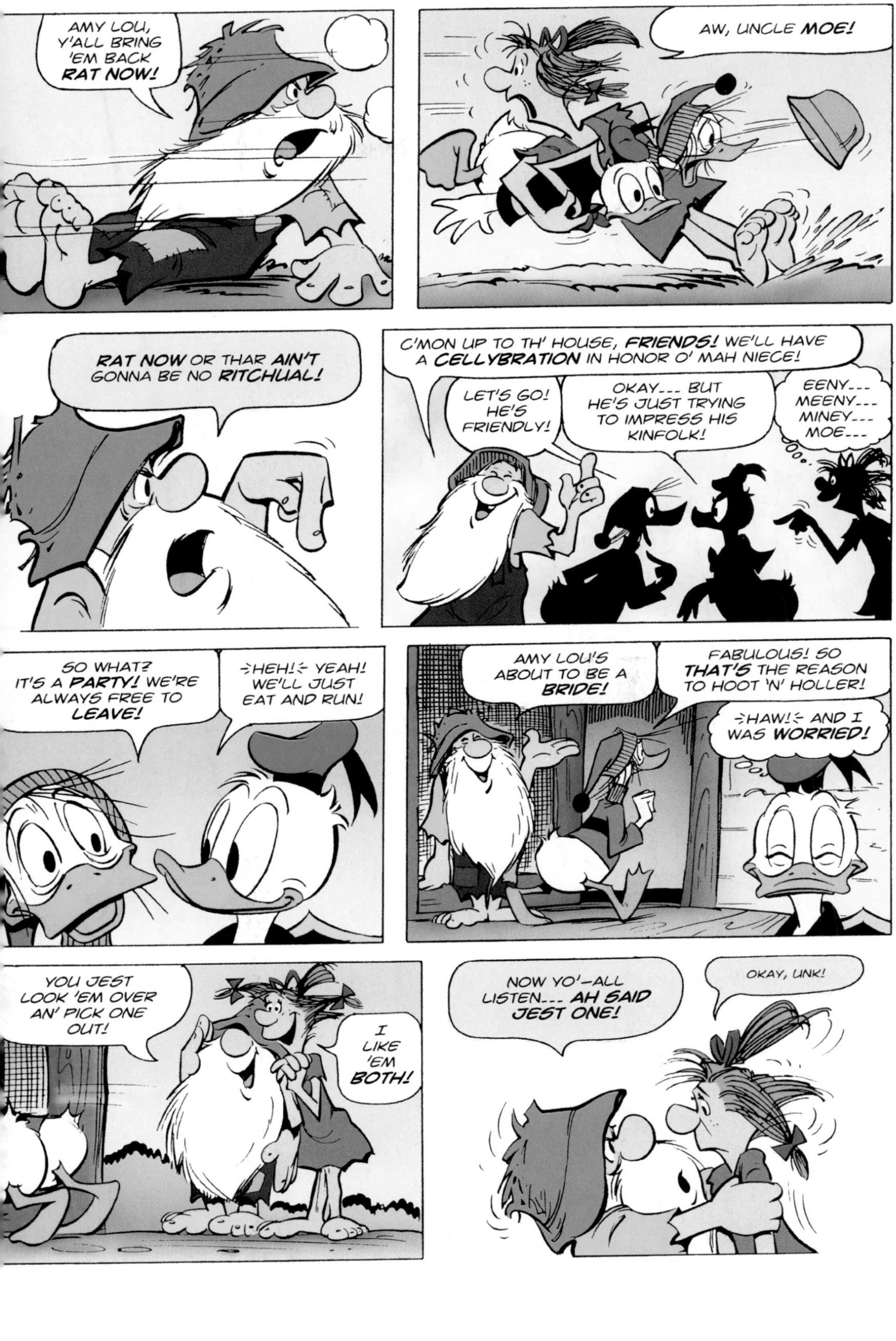
AMY LOU, Y'ALL BRING 'EM BACK RAT NOW!
AW, UNCLE MOE!
RAT NOW OR THAR AIN'T GONNA BE NO RITCHUAL!
C'MON UP TO TH' HOUSE, FRIENDS! WE'LL HAVE A CELLYBRATION IN HONOR O' MAH NIECE!
LET'S GO! HE'S FRIENDLY!
OKAY--- BUT HE'S JUST TRYING TO IMPRESS HIS KINFOLK!
EENY--- MEENY--- MINEY--- MOE---
SO WHAT? IT'S A PARTY! WE'RE ALWAYS FREE TO LEAVE!
HEH! YEAH! WE'LL JUST EAT AND RUN!
AMY LOU'S ABOUT TO BE A BRIDE!
FABULOUS! SO THAT'S THE REASON TO HOOT 'N' HOLLER!
HAW! AND I WAS WORRIED!
YOU JEST LOOK 'EM OVER AN' PICK ONE OUT!
I LIKE 'EM BOTH!
NOW YO'-ALL LISTEN--- AH SAID JEST ONE!
OKAY, UNK!

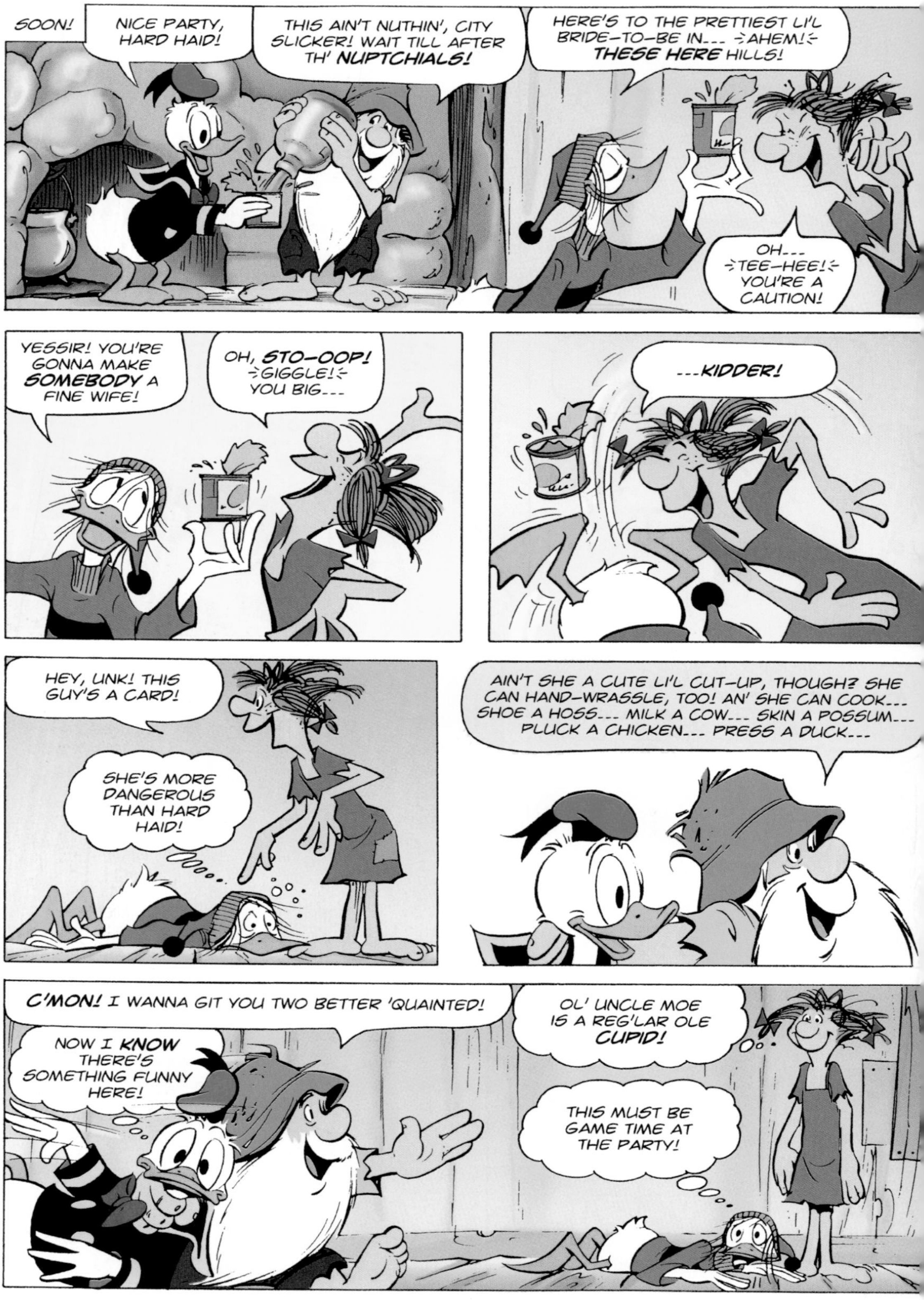
SOON!
NICE PARTY, HARD HAID!
THIS AIN'T NUTHIN', CITY SLICKER! WAIT TILL AFTER TH' NUPTCHIALS!
HERE'S TO THE PRETTIEST LI'L BRIDE-TO-BE IN--- AHEM! THESE HERE HILLS!
OH--- TEE-HEE! YOU'RE A CAUTION!
YESSIR! YOU'RE GONNA MAKE SOMEBODY A FINE WIFE!
OH, STO-OOP! GIGGLE! YOU BIG---
---KIDDER!
HEY, UNK! THIS GUY'S A CARD!
SHE'S MORE DANGEROUS THAN HARD HAID!
AIN'T SHE A CUTE LI'L CUT-UP, THOUGH? SHE CAN HAND-WRASSLE, TOO! AN' SHE CAN COOK--- SHOE A HOSS--- MILK A COW--- SKIN A POSSUM--- PLUCK A CHICKEN--- PRESS A DUCK---
C'MON! I WANNA GIT YOU TWO BETTER 'QUAINTED!
NOW I KNOW THERE'S SOMETHING FUNNY HERE!
OL' UNCLE MOE IS A REG'LAR OLE CUPID!
THIS MUST BE GAME TIME AT THE PARTY!

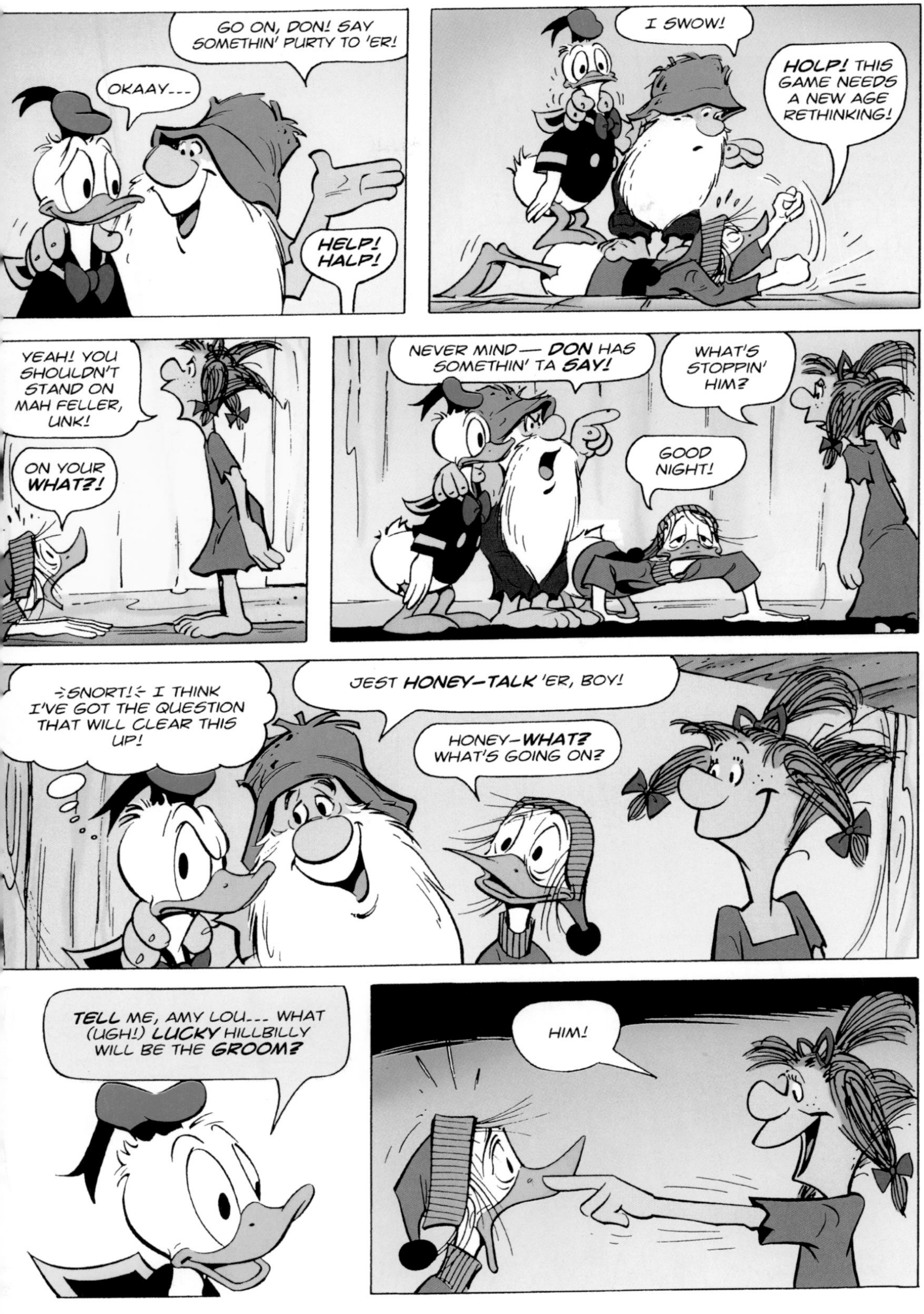
GO ON, DON! SAY SOMETHIN' PURTY TO 'ER!
OKAAY---
HELP! HALP!
I SWOW!
HOLP! THIS GAME NEEDS A NEW AGE RETHINKING!
YEAH! YOU SHOULDN'T STAND ON MAH FELLER, UNK!
ON YOUR WHAT?!
NEVER MIND— DON HAS SOMETHIN' TA SAY!
WHAT'S STOPPIN' HIM?
GOOD NIGHT!
SNORT! I THINK I'VE GOT THE QUESTION THAT WILL CLEAR THIS UP!
JEST HONEY-TALK 'ER, BOY!
HONEY-WHAT? WHAT'S GOING ON?
TELL ME, AMY LOU--- WHAT (UGH!) LUCKY HILLBILLY WILL BE THE GROOM?
HIM!

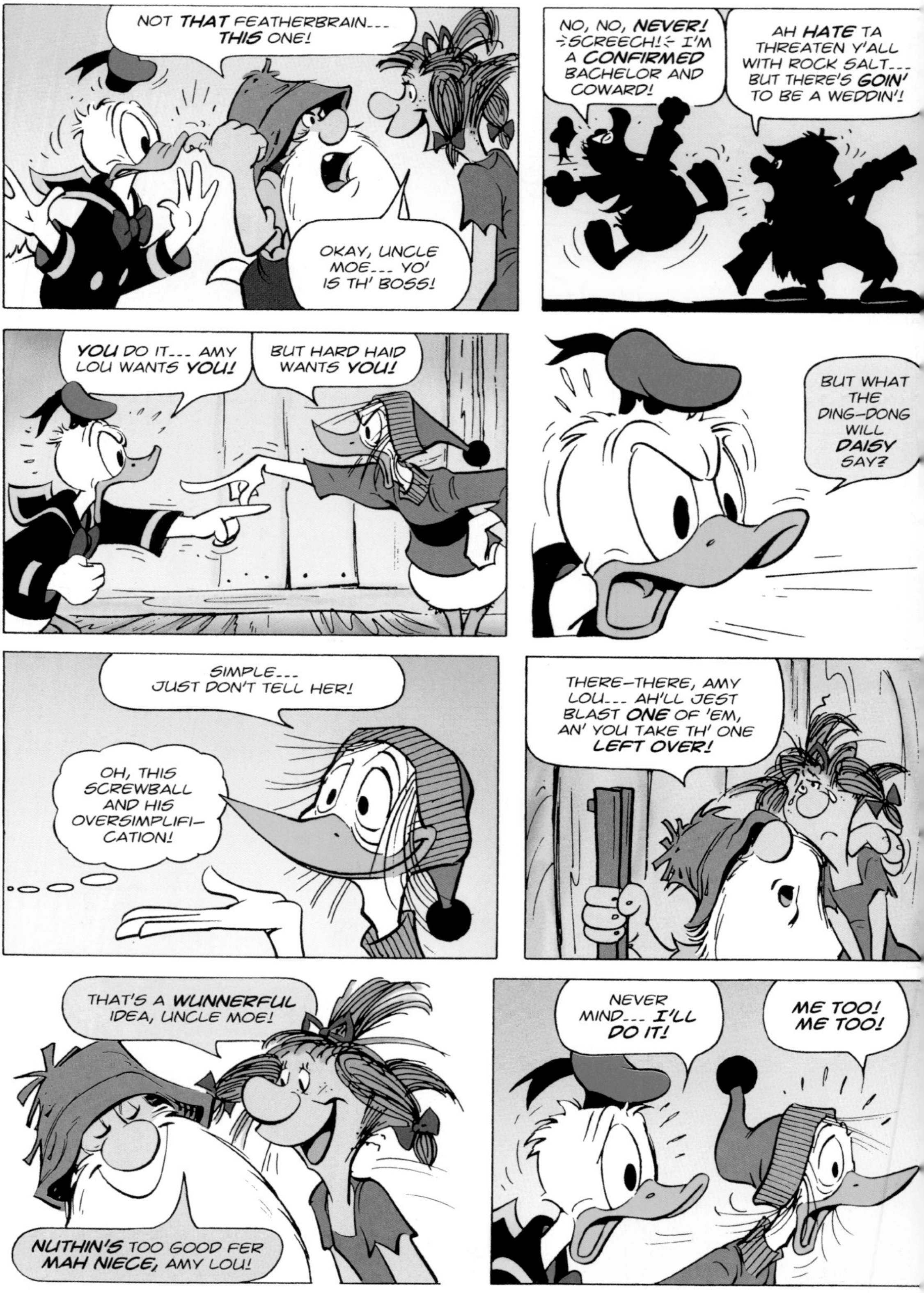
NOT THAT FEATHERBRAIN--- THIS ONE!
OKAY, UNCLE MOE--- YO' IS TH' BOSS!
NO, NO, NEVER! ≈SCREECH!≈ I'M A CONFIRMED BACHELOR AND COWARD!
AH HATE TA THREATEN Y'ALL WITH ROCK SALT--- BUT THERE'S GOIN' TO BE A WEDDIN'!
YOU DO IT--- AMY LOU WANTS YOU!
BUT HARD HAID WANTS YOU!
BUT WHAT THE DING-DONG WILL DAISY SAY?
SIMPLE--- JUST DON'T TELL HER!
OH, THIS SCREWBALL AND HIS OVERSIMPLIFI-CATION!
THERE-THERE, AMY LOU--- AH'LL JEST BLAST ONE OF 'EM, AN' YOU TAKE TH' ONE LEFT OVER!
THAT'S A WUNNERFUL IDEA, UNCLE MOE!
NUTHIN'S TOO GOOD FER MAH NIECE, AMY LOU!
NEVER MIND--- I'LL DO IT!
ME TOO! ME TOO!

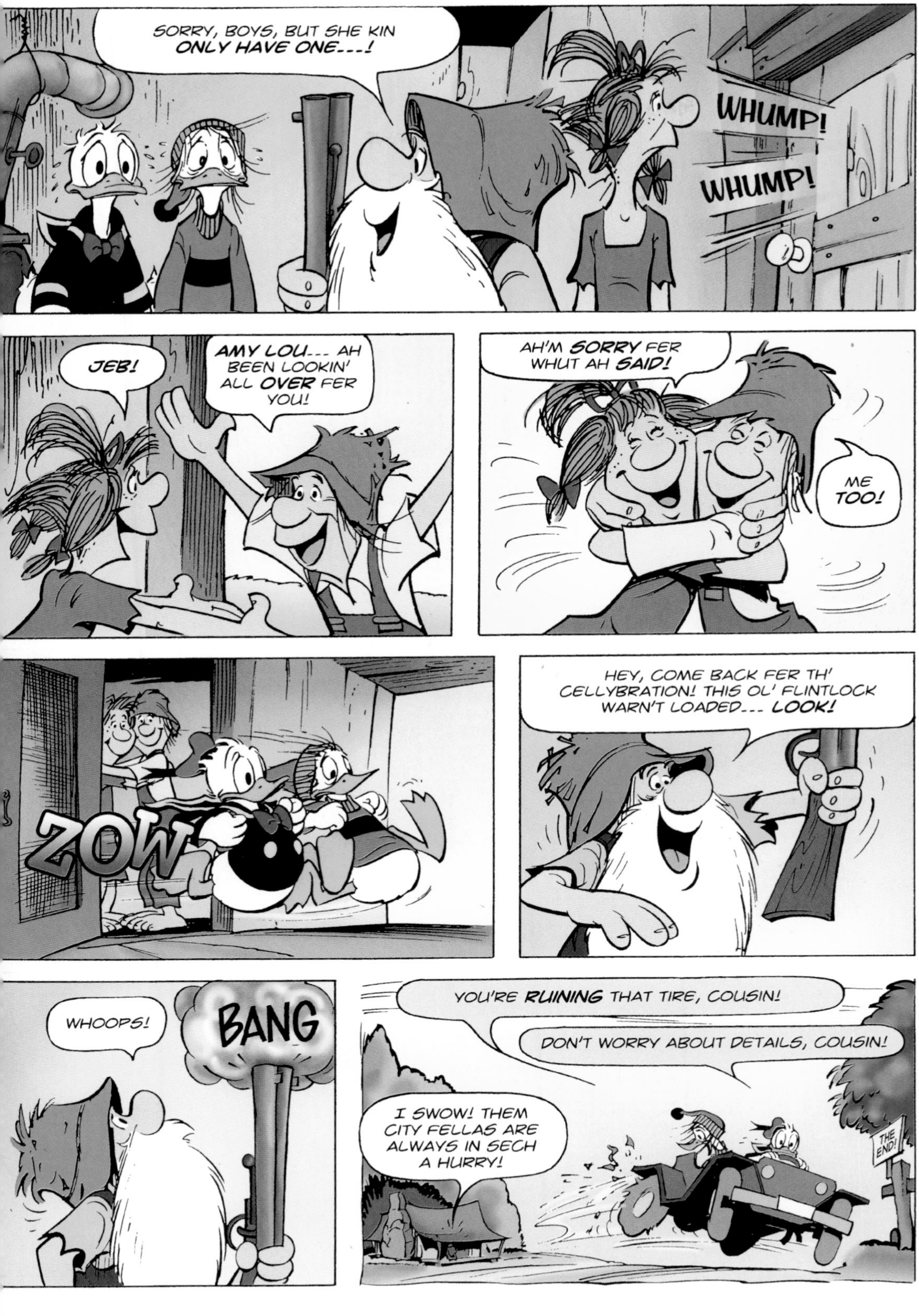
SORRY, BOYS, BUT SHE KIN **ONLY HAVE ONE---!**
WHUMP!
WHUMP!
JEB!
AMY LOU--- AH BEEN LOOKIN' ALL **OVER** FER YOU!
AH'M **SORRY** FER WHUT AH **SAID!**
ME **TOO!**
ZOW
HEY, COME BACK FER TH' CELLYBRATION! THIS OL' FLINTLOCK WARN'T LOADED--- **LOOK!**
WHOOPS!
BANG
YOU'RE **RUINING** THAT TIRE, COUSIN!
DON'T WORRY ABOUT DETAILS, COUSIN!
I SWOW! THEM CITY FELLAS ARE ALWAYS IN SECH A HURRY!
THE END!

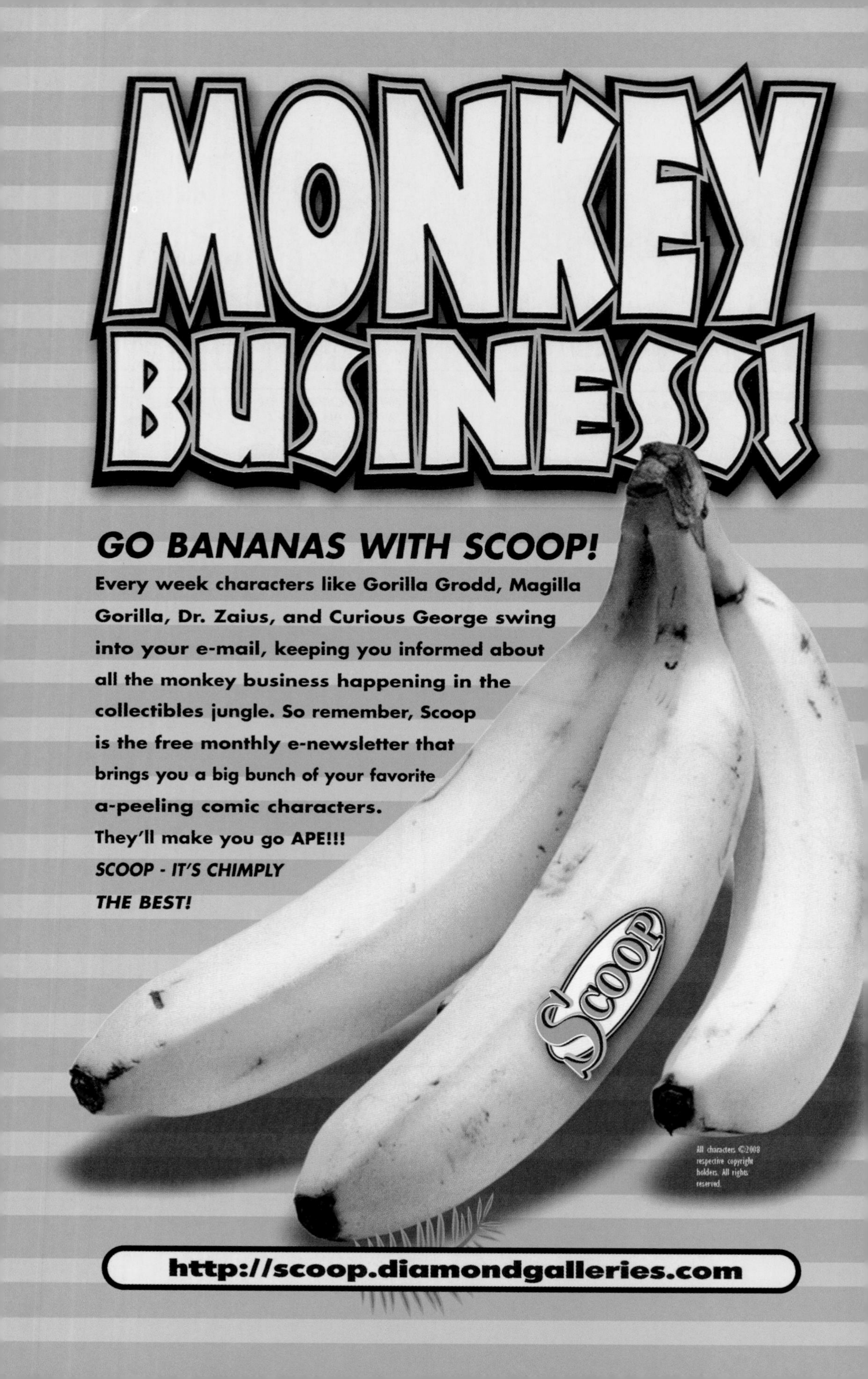
MONKEY BUSINESS!
GO BANANAS WITH SCOOP!
Every week characters like Gorilla Grodd, Magilla Gorilla, Dr. Zaius, and Curious George swing into your e-mail, keeping you informed about all the monkey business happening in the collectibles jungle. So remember, Scoop is the free monthly e-newsletter that brings you a big bunch of your favorite a-peeling comic characters.
They'll make you go APE!!!
SCOOP - IT'S CHIMPLY THE BEST!
SCOOP
All characters ©2008 respective copyright holders. All rights reserved.
http://scoop.diamondgalleries.com

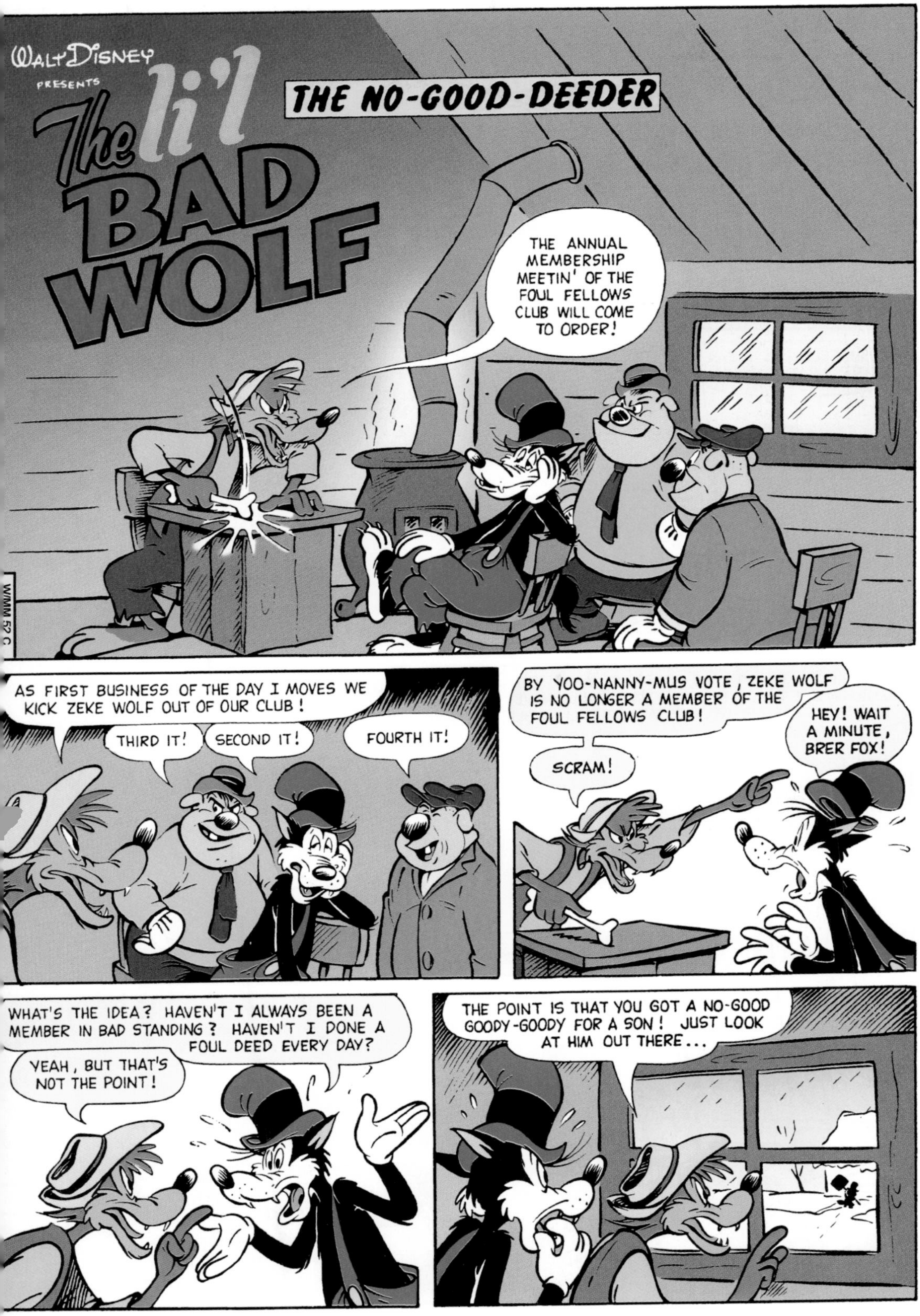
WALT DISNEY
PRESENTS
The li'l BAD WOLF
THE NO-GOOD-DEEDER
THE ANNUAL MEMBERSHIP MEETIN' OF THE FOUL FELLOWS CLUB WILL COME TO ORDER!
AS FIRST BUSINESS OF THE DAY I MOVES WE KICK ZEKE WOLF OUT OF OUR CLUB!
THIRD IT!
SECOND IT!
FOURTH IT!
BY YOO-NANNY-MUS VOTE, ZEKE WOLF IS NO LONGER A MEMBER OF THE FOUL FELLOWS CLUB!
SCRAM!
HEY! WAIT A MINUTE, BRER FOX!
WHAT'S THE IDEA? HAVEN'T I ALWAYS BEEN A MEMBER IN BAD STANDING? HAVEN'T I DONE A FOUL DEED EVERY DAY?
YEAH, BUT THAT'S NOT THE POINT!
THE POINT IS THAT YOU GOT A NO-GOOD GOODY-GOODY FOR A SON! JUST LOOK AT HIM OUT THERE...
WIMM 52 C

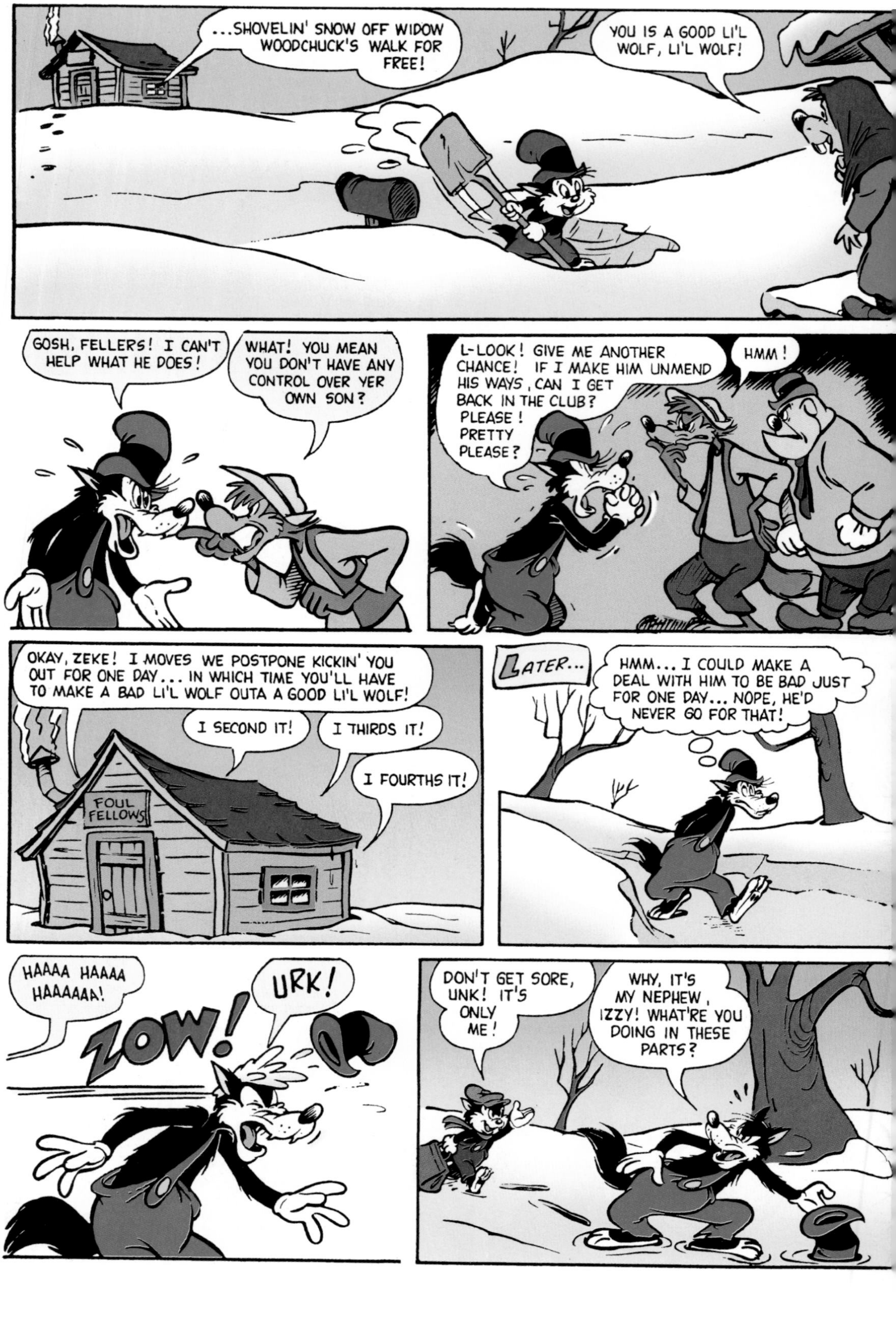
...SHOVELIN' SNOW OFF WIDOW WOODCHUCK'S WALK FOR FREE!
YOU IS A GOOD LI'L WOLF, LI'L WOLF!
GOSH, FELLERS! I CAN'T HELP WHAT HE DOES!
WHAT! YOU MEAN YOU DON'T HAVE ANY CONTROL OVER YER OWN SON?
L-LOOK! GIVE ME ANOTHER CHANCE! IF I MAKE HIM UNMEND HIS WAYS, CAN I GET BACK IN THE CLUB? PLEASE! PRETTY PLEASE?
HMM!
OKAY, ZEKE! I MOVES WE POSTPONE KICKIN' YOU OUT FOR ONE DAY... IN WHICH TIME YOU'LL HAVE TO MAKE A BAD LI'L WOLF OUTA A GOOD LI'L WOLF!
I SECOND IT!
I THIRDS IT!
I FOURTHS IT!
FOUL FELLOWS
LATER...
HMM... I COULD MAKE A DEAL WITH HIM TO BE BAD JUST FOR ONE DAY... NOPE, HE'D NEVER GO FOR THAT!
HAAAA HAAAA HAAAAAA!
ZOW!
URK!
DON'T GET SORE, UNK! IT'S ONLY ME!
WHY, IT'S MY NEPHEW, IZZY! WHAT'RE YOU DOING IN THESE PARTS?

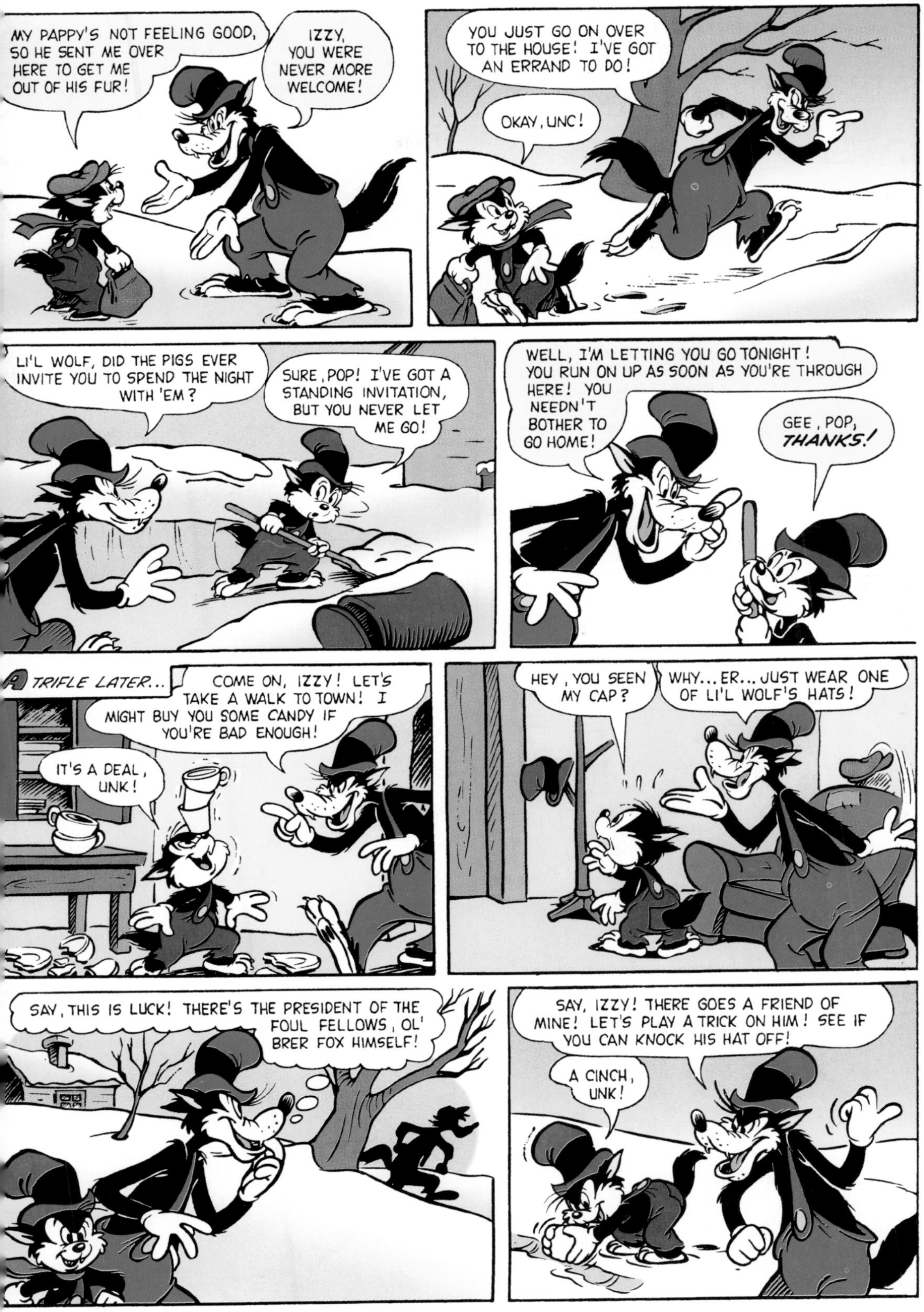
MY PAPPY'S NOT FEELING GOOD, SO HE SENT ME OVER HERE TO GET ME OUT OF HIS FUR!
IZZY, YOU WERE NEVER MORE WELCOME!
YOU JUST GO ON OVER TO THE HOUSE! I'VE GOT AN ERRAND TO DO!
OKAY, UNC!
LI'L WOLF, DID THE PIGS EVER INVITE YOU TO SPEND THE NIGHT WITH 'EM?
SURE, POP! I'VE GOT A STANDING INVITATION, BUT YOU NEVER LET ME GO!
WELL, I'M LETTING YOU GO TONIGHT! YOU RUN ON UP AS SOON AS YOU'RE THROUGH HERE! YOU NEEDN'T BOTHER TO GO HOME!
GEE, POP, THANKS!
A TRIFLE LATER...
COME ON, IZZY! LET'S TAKE A WALK TO TOWN! I MIGHT BUY YOU SOME CANDY IF YOU'RE BAD ENOUGH!
IT'S A DEAL, UNK!
HEY, YOU SEEN MY CAP?
WHY... ER... JUST WEAR ONE OF LI'L WOLF'S HATS!
SAY, THIS IS LUCK! THERE'S THE PRESIDENT OF THE FOUL FELLOWS, OL' BRER FOX HIMSELF!
SAY, IZZY! THERE GOES A FRIEND OF MINE! LET'S PLAY A TRICK ON HIM! SEE IF YOU CAN KNOCK HIS HAT OFF!
A CINCH, UNK!

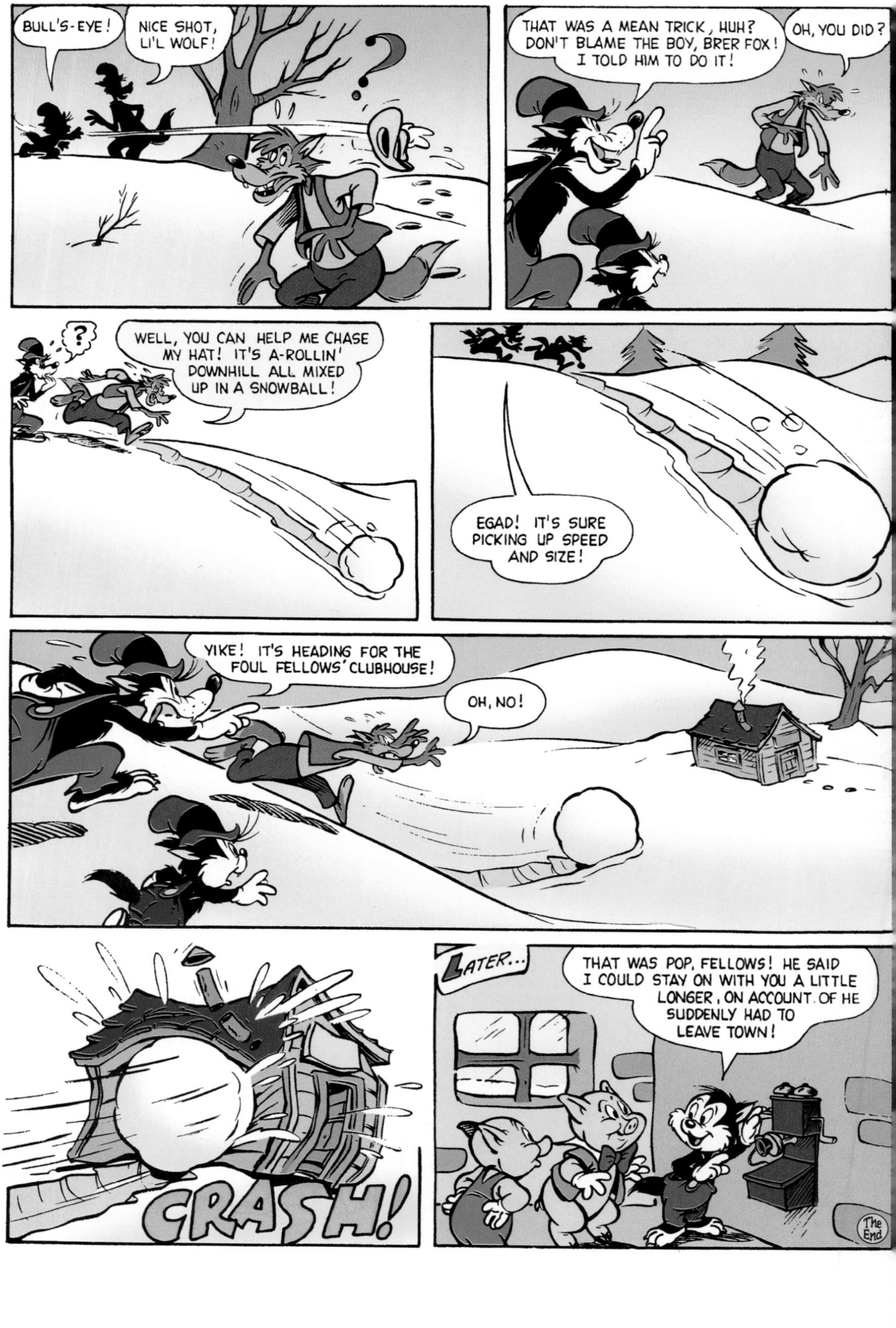
BULL'S-EYE!
NICE SHOT, LI'L WOLF!
?
THAT WAS A MEAN TRICK, HUH? DON'T BLAME THE BOY, BRER FOX! I TOLD HIM TO DO IT!
OH, YOU DID?
?
WELL, YOU CAN HELP ME CHASE MY HAT! IT'S A-ROLLIN' DOWNHILL ALL MIXED UP IN A SNOWBALL!
EGAD! IT'S SURE PICKING UP SPEED AND SIZE!
YIKE! IT'S HEADING FOR THE FOUL FELLOWS' CLUBHOUSE!
OH, NO!
CRASH!
LATER...
THAT WAS POP, FELLOWS! HE SAID I COULD STAY ON WITH YOU A LITTLE LONGER, ON ACCOUNT OF HE SUDDENLY HAD TO LEAVE TOWN!
The End

Walt Disney's MICKEY MOUSE in SCHOOLGIRLS

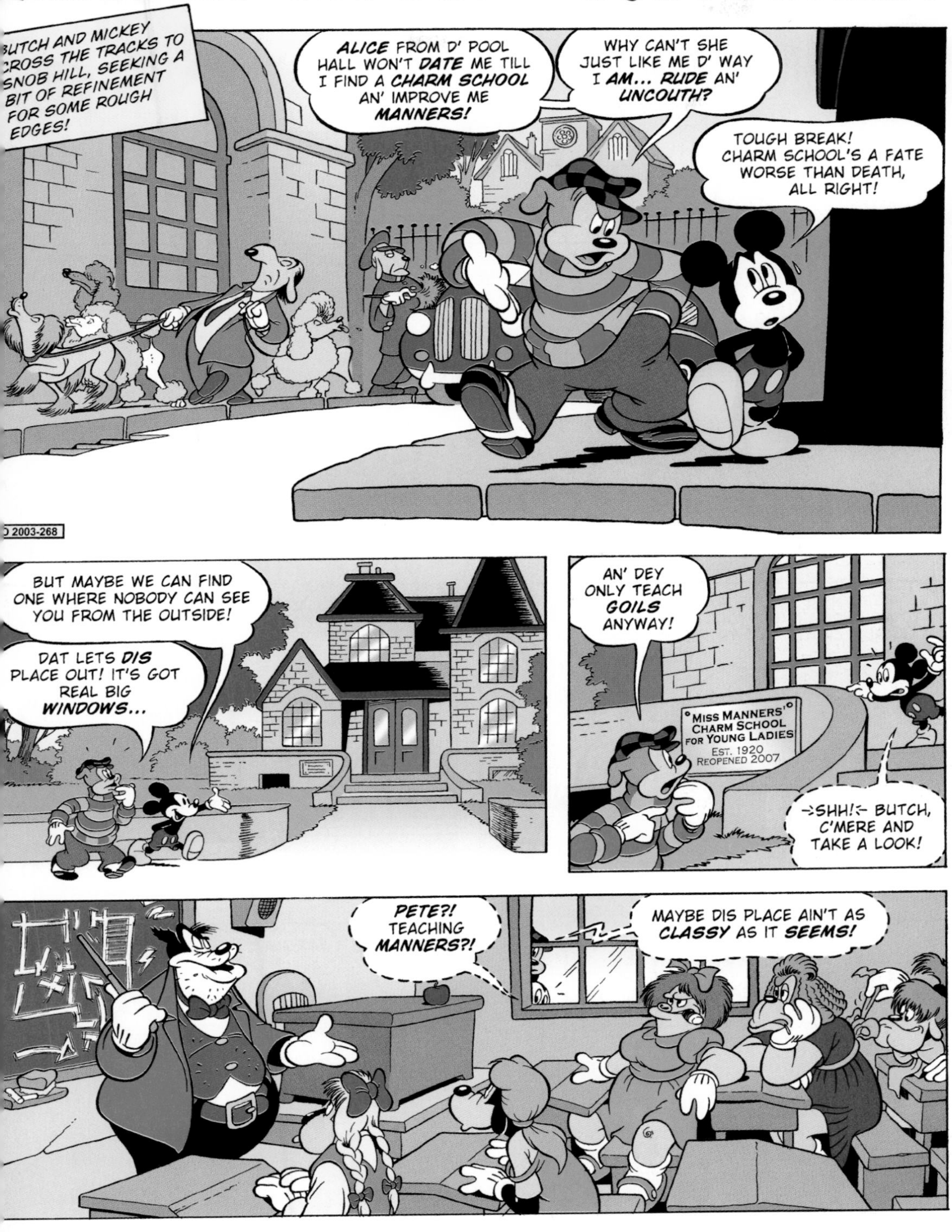
BUTCH AND MICKEY CROSS THE TRACKS TO SNOB HILL, SEEKING A BIT OF REFINEMENT FOR SOME ROUGH EDGES!
ALICE FROM D' POOL HALL WON'T DATE ME TILL I FIND A CHARM SCHOOL AN' IMPROVE ME MANNERS!
WHY CAN'T SHE JUST LIKE ME D' WAY I AM... RUDE AN' UNCOUTH?
TOUGH BREAK! CHARM SCHOOL'S A FATE WORSE THAN DEATH, ALL RIGHT!
D 2003-268
BUT MAYBE WE CAN FIND ONE WHERE NOBODY CAN SEE YOU FROM THE OUTSIDE!
DAT LETS DIS PLACE OUT! IT'S GOT REAL BIG WINDOWS...
AN' DEY ONLY TEACH GOILS ANYWAY!
MISS MANNERS' CHARM SCHOOL FOR YOUNG LADIES EST. 1920 REOPENED 2007
→SHH!← BUTCH, C'MERE AND TAKE A LOOK!
PETE?! TEACHING MANNERS?!
MAYBE DIS PLACE AIN'T AS CLASSY AS IT SEEMS!

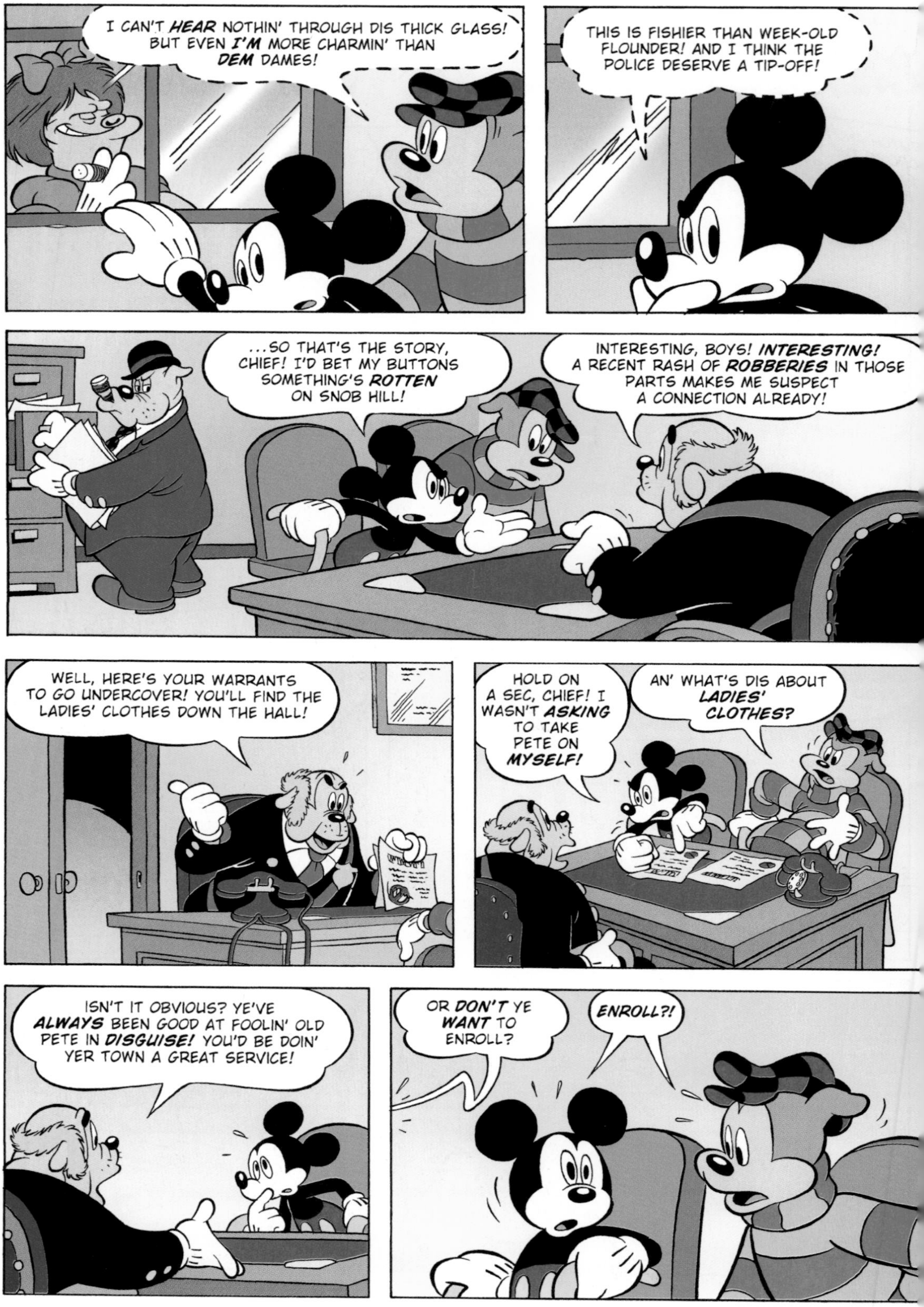
I CAN'T HEAR NOTHIN' THROUGH DIS THICK GLASS! BUT EVEN I'M MORE CHARMIN' THAN DEM DAMES!
THIS IS FISHIER THAN WEEK-OLD FLOUNDER! AND I THINK THE POLICE DESERVE A TIP-OFF!
...SO THAT'S THE STORY, CHIEF! I'D BET MY BUTTONS SOMETHING'S ROTTEN ON SNOB HILL!
INTERESTING, BOYS! INTERESTING! A RECENT RASH OF ROBBERIES IN THOSE PARTS MAKES ME SUSPECT A CONNECTION ALREADY!
WELL, HERE'S YOUR WARRANTS TO GO UNDERCOVER! YOU'LL FIND THE LADIES' CLOTHES DOWN THE HALL!
HOLD ON A SEC, CHIEF! I WASN'T ASKING TO TAKE PETE ON MYSELF!
AN' WHAT'S DIS ABOUT LADIES' CLOTHES?
ISN'T IT OBVIOUS? YE'VE ALWAYS BEEN GOOD AT FOOLIN' OLD PETE IN DISGUISE! YOU'D BE DOIN' YER TOWN A GREAT SERVICE!
OR DON'T YE WANT TO ENROLL?
ENROLL?!

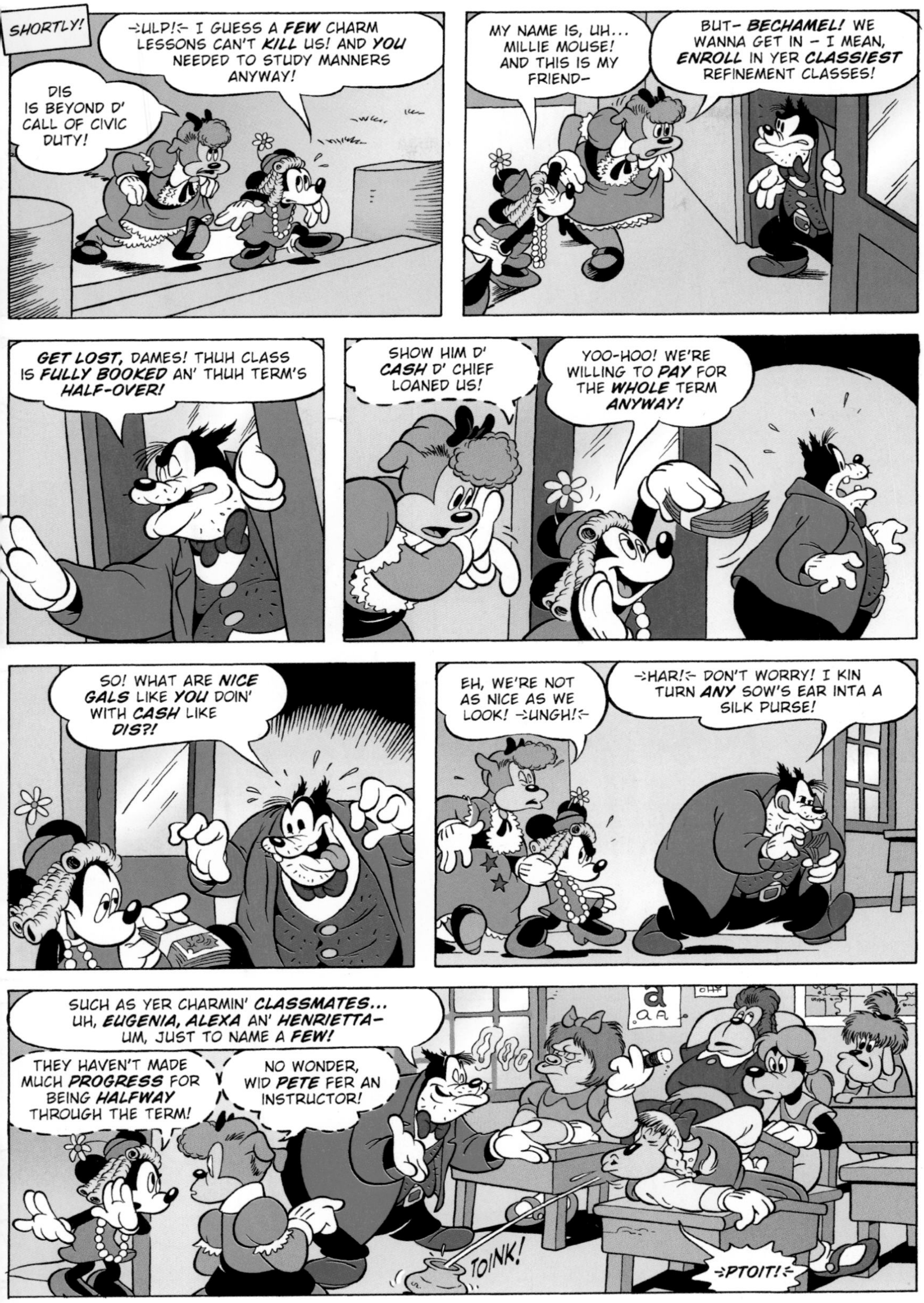
SHORTLY!
DIS IS BEYOND D' CALL OF CIVIC DUTY!
→ULP!← I GUESS A FEW CHARM LESSONS CAN'T KILL US! AND YOU NEEDED TO STUDY MANNERS ANYWAY!
MY NAME IS, UH... MILLIE MOUSE! AND THIS IS MY FRIEND—
BUT— BECHAMEL! WE WANNA GET IN — I MEAN, ENROLL IN YER CLASSIEST REFINEMENT CLASSES!
GET LOST, DAMES! THUH CLASS IS FULLY BOOKED AN' THUH TERM'S HALF-OVER!
SHOW HIM D' CASH D' CHIEF LOANED US!
YOO-HOO! WE'RE WILLING TO PAY FOR THE WHOLE TERM ANYWAY!
SO! WHAT ARE NICE GALS LIKE YOU DOIN' WITH CASH LIKE DIS?!
EH, WE'RE NOT AS NICE AS WE LOOK! →UNGH!←
→HAR!← DON'T WORRY! I KIN TURN ANY SOW'S EAR INTA A SILK PURSE!
SUCH AS YER CHARMIN' CLASSMATES... UH, EUGENIA, ALEXA AN' HENRIETTA— UM, JUST TO NAME A FEW!
THEY HAVEN'T MADE MUCH PROGRESS FOR BEING HALFWAY THROUGH THE TERM!
NO WONDER, WID PETE FER AN INSTRUCTOR!
TOINK!
→PTOIT!←

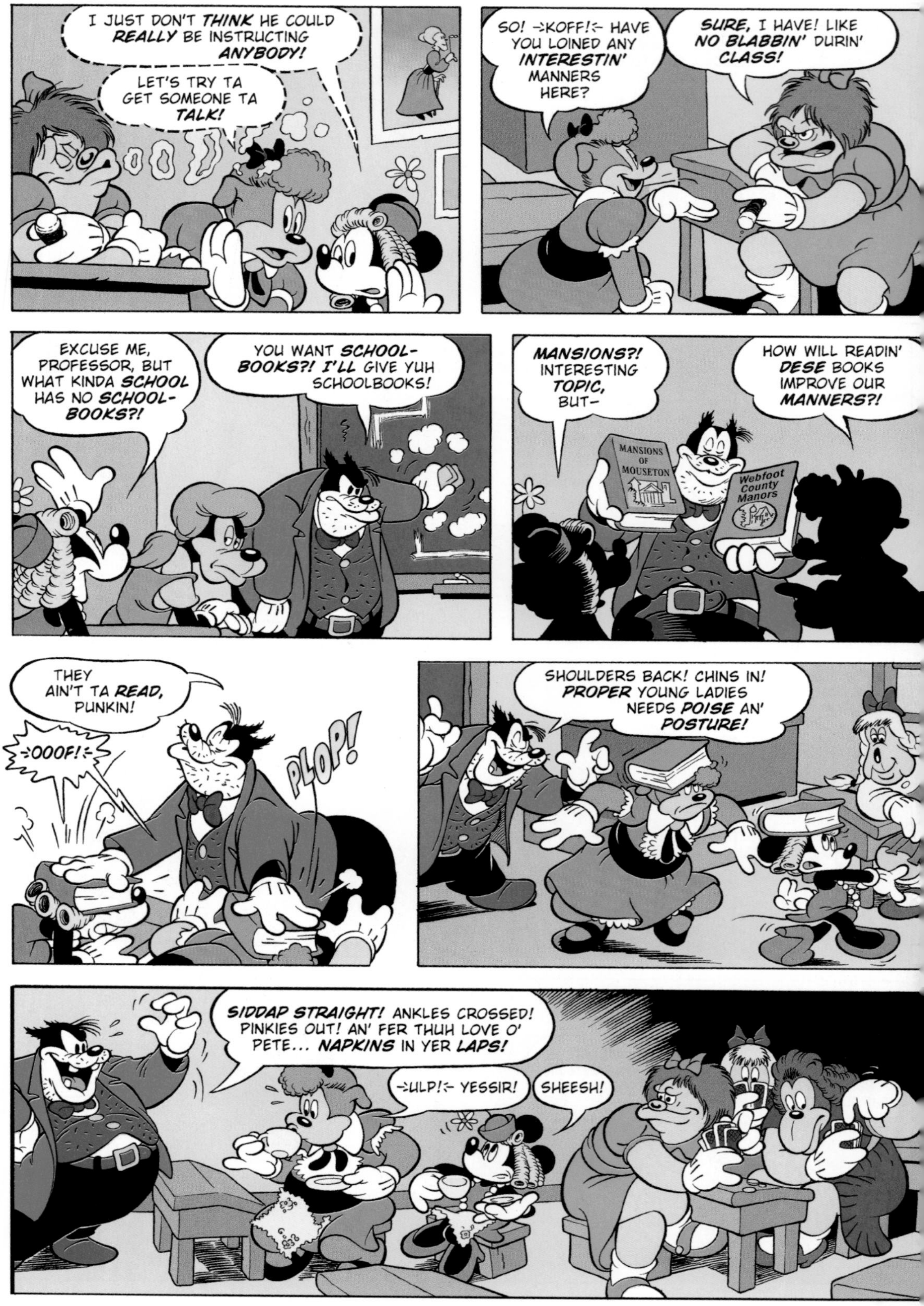
I JUST DON'T THINK HE COULD REALLY BE INSTRUCTING ANYBODY!
LET'S TRY TA GET SOMEONE TA TALK!
SO! -KOFF!- HAVE YOU LOINED ANY INTERESTIN' MANNERS HERE?
SURE, I HAVE! LIKE NO BLABBIN' DURIN' CLASS!
EXCUSE ME, PROFESSOR, BUT WHAT KINDA SCHOOL HAS NO SCHOOL-BOOKS?!
YOU WANT SCHOOL-BOOKS?! I'LL GIVE YUH SCHOOLBOOKS!
MANSIONS?! INTERESTING TOPIC, BUT-
HOW WILL READIN' DESE BOOKS IMPROVE OUR MANNERS?!
MANSIONS OF MOUSETON
Webfoot County Manors
THEY AIN'T TA READ, PUNKIN!
-OOOF!-
PLOP!
SHOULDERS BACK! CHINS IN! PROPER YOUNG LADIES NEEDS POISE AN' POSTURE!
SIDDAP STRAIGHT! ANKLES CROSSED! PINKIES OUT! AN' FER THUH LOVE O' PETE... NAPKINS IN YER LAPS!
-ULP!- YESSIR!
SHEESH!

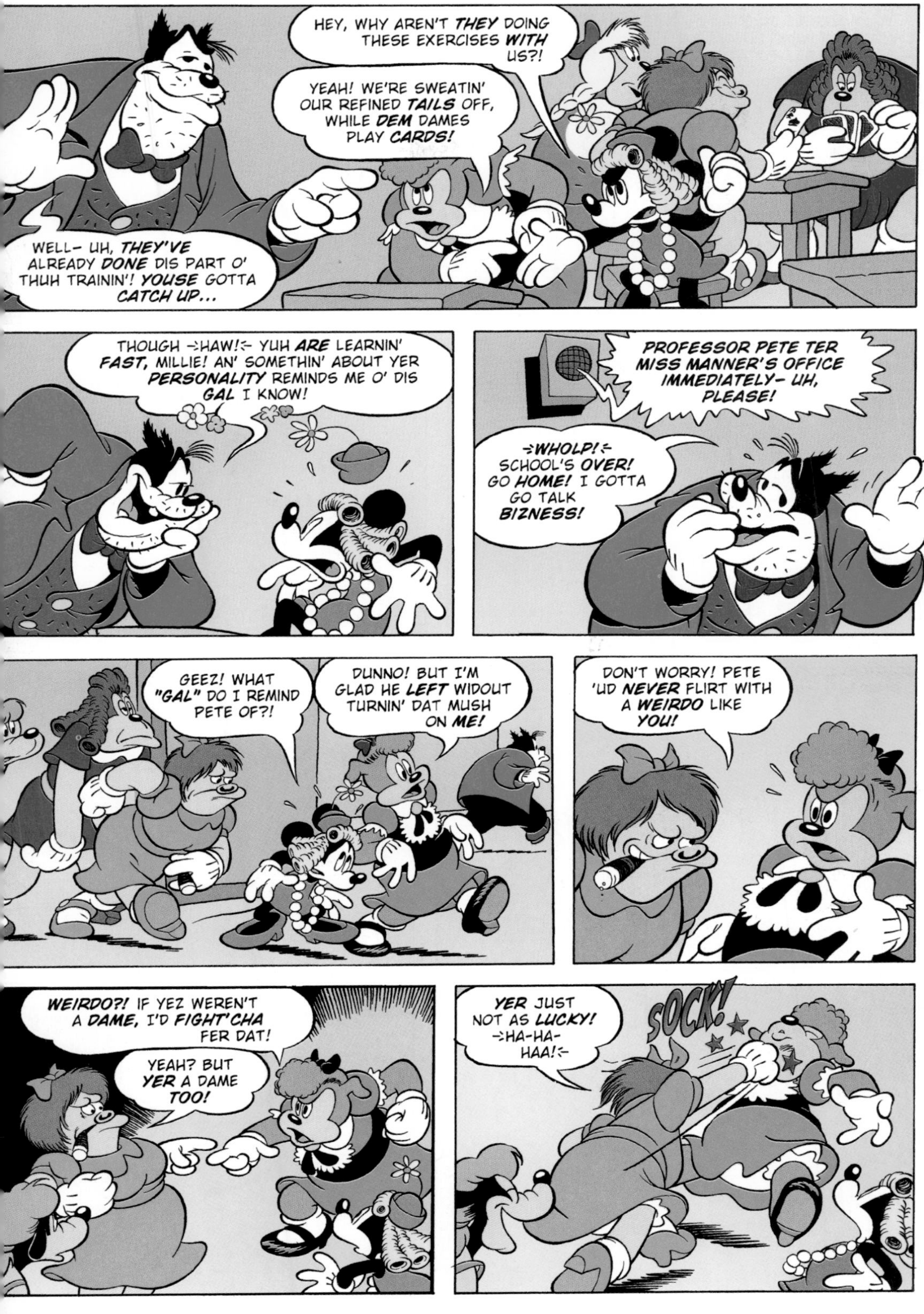
HEY, WHY AREN'T THEY DOING THESE EXERCISES WITH US?!
YEAH! WE'RE SWEATIN' OUR REFINED TAILS OFF, WHILE DEM DAMES PLAY CARDS!
WELL- UH, THEY'VE ALREADY DONE DIS PART O' THUH TRAININ'! YOUSE GOTTA CATCH UP...
THOUGH -HAW!- YUH ARE LEARNIN' FAST, MILLIE! AN' SOMETHIN' ABOUT YER PERSONALITY REMINDS ME O' DIS GAL I KNOW!
PROFESSOR PETE TER MISS MANNER'S OFFICE IMMEDIATELY- UH, PLEASE!
-WHOLP!- SCHOOL'S OVER! GO HOME! I GOTTA GO TALK BIZNESS!
GEEZ! WHAT "GAL" DO I REMIND PETE OF?!
DUNNO! BUT I'M GLAD HE LEFT WIDOUT TURNIN' DAT MUSH ON ME!
DON'T WORRY! PETE 'UD NEVER FLIRT WITH A WEIRDO LIKE YOU!
WEIRDO?! IF YEZ WEREN'T A DAME, I'D FIGHT'CHA FER DAT!
YEAH? BUT YER A DAME TOO!
YER JUST NOT AS LUCKY! -HA-HA-HAA!-
SOCK!

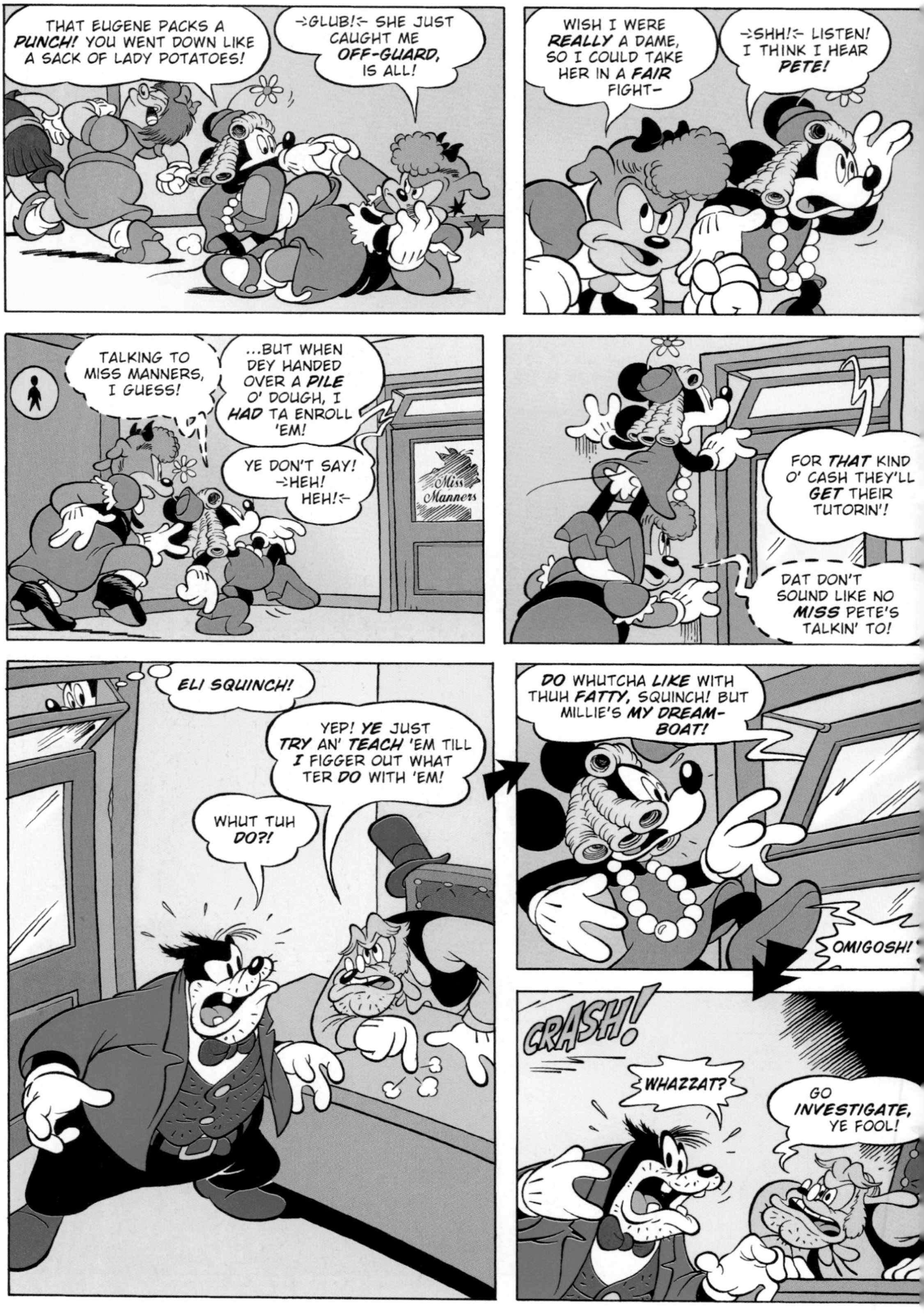
THAT EUGENE PACKS A PUNCH! YOU WENT DOWN LIKE A SACK OF LADY POTATOES!
-GLUB!- SHE JUST CAUGHT ME OFF-GUARD, IS ALL!
WISH I WERE REALLY A DAME, SO I COULD TAKE HER IN A FAIR FIGHT—
-SHH!- LISTEN! I THINK I HEAR PETE!
TALKING TO MISS MANNERS, I GUESS!
...BUT WHEN DEY HANDED OVER A PILE O' DOUGH, I HAD TA ENROLL 'EM!
YE DON'T SAY! -HEH! HEH!-
Miss Manners
FOR THAT KIND O' CASH THEY'LL GET THEIR TUTORIN'!
DAT DON'T SOUND LIKE NO MISS PETE'S TALKIN' TO!
ELI SQUINCH!
YEP! YE JUST TRY AN' TEACH 'EM TILL I FIGGER OUT WHAT TER DO WITH 'EM!
WHUT TUH DO?!
DO WHUTCHA LIKE WITH THUH FATTY, SQUINCH! BUT MILLIE'S MY DREAM-BOAT!
OMIGOSH!
CRASH!
WHAZZAT?
GO INVESTIGATE, YE FOOL!

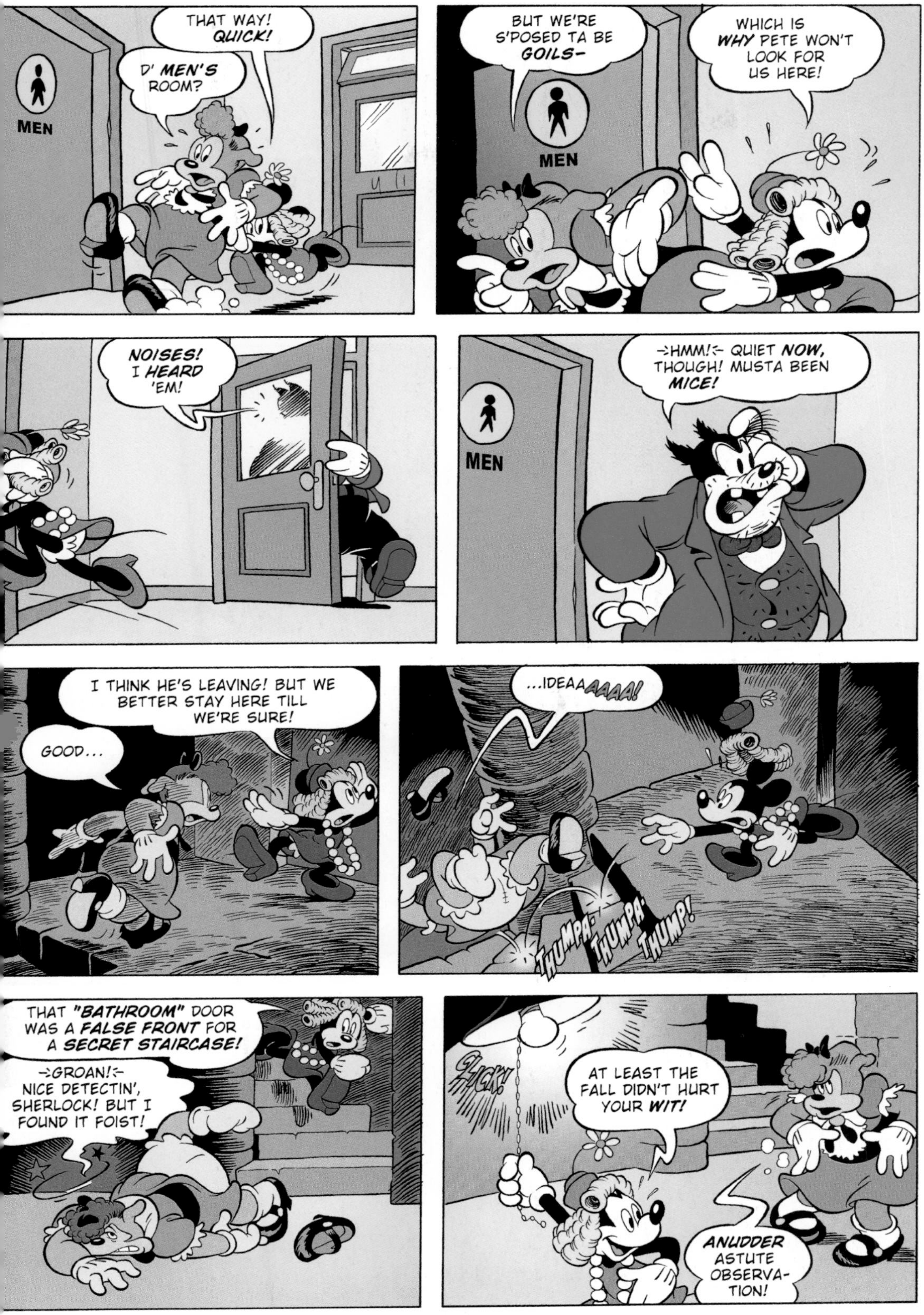
MEN
THAT WAY! QUICK!
D' MEN'S ROOM?
MEN
BUT WE'RE S'POSED TA BE GOILS–
WHICH IS WHY PETE WON'T LOOK FOR US HERE!
NOISES! I HEARD 'EM!
MEN
–HMM!– QUIET NOW, THOUGH! MUSTA BEEN MICE!
I THINK HE'S LEAVING! BUT WE BETTER STAY HERE TILL WE'RE SURE!
GOOD...
...IDEAAAAAA!
THUMPA-THUMPA-THUMP!
THAT "BATHROOM" DOOR WAS A FALSE FRONT FOR A SECRET STAIRCASE!
–GROAN!– NICE DETECTIN', SHERLOCK! BUT I FOUND IT FOIST!
CLICK!
AT LEAST THE FALL DIDN'T HURT YOUR WIT!
ANUDDER ASTUTE OBSERVA-TION!

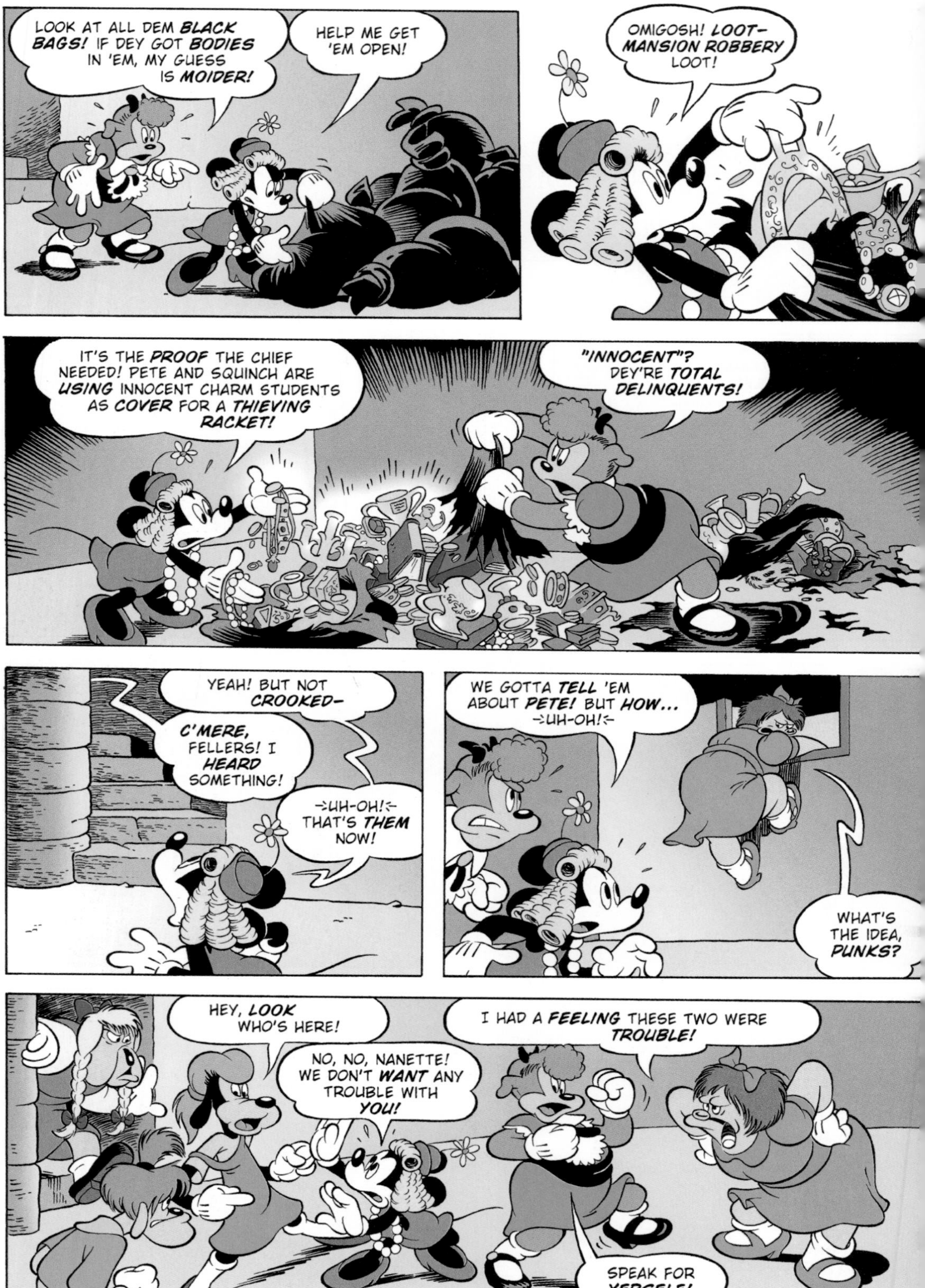
LOOK AT ALL DEM BLACK BAGS! IF DEY GOT BODIES IN 'EM, MY GUESS IS MOIDER!
HELP ME GET 'EM OPEN!
OMIGOSH! LOOT— MANSION ROBBERY LOOT!
IT'S THE PROOF THE CHIEF NEEDED! PETE AND SQUINCH ARE USING INNOCENT CHARM STUDENTS AS COVER FOR A THIEVING RACKET!
"INNOCENT"? DEY'RE TOTAL DELINQUENTS!
YEAH! BUT NOT CROOKED—
C'MERE, FELLERS! I HEARD SOMETHING!
UH-OH! THAT'S THEM NOW!
WE GOTTA TELL 'EM ABOUT PETE! BUT HOW... UH-OH!
WHAT'S THE IDEA, PUNKS?
HEY, LOOK WHO'S HERE!
NO, NO, NANETTE! WE DON'T WANT ANY TROUBLE WITH YOU!
I HAD A FEELING THESE TWO WERE TROUBLE!
SPEAK FOR YERSELF!

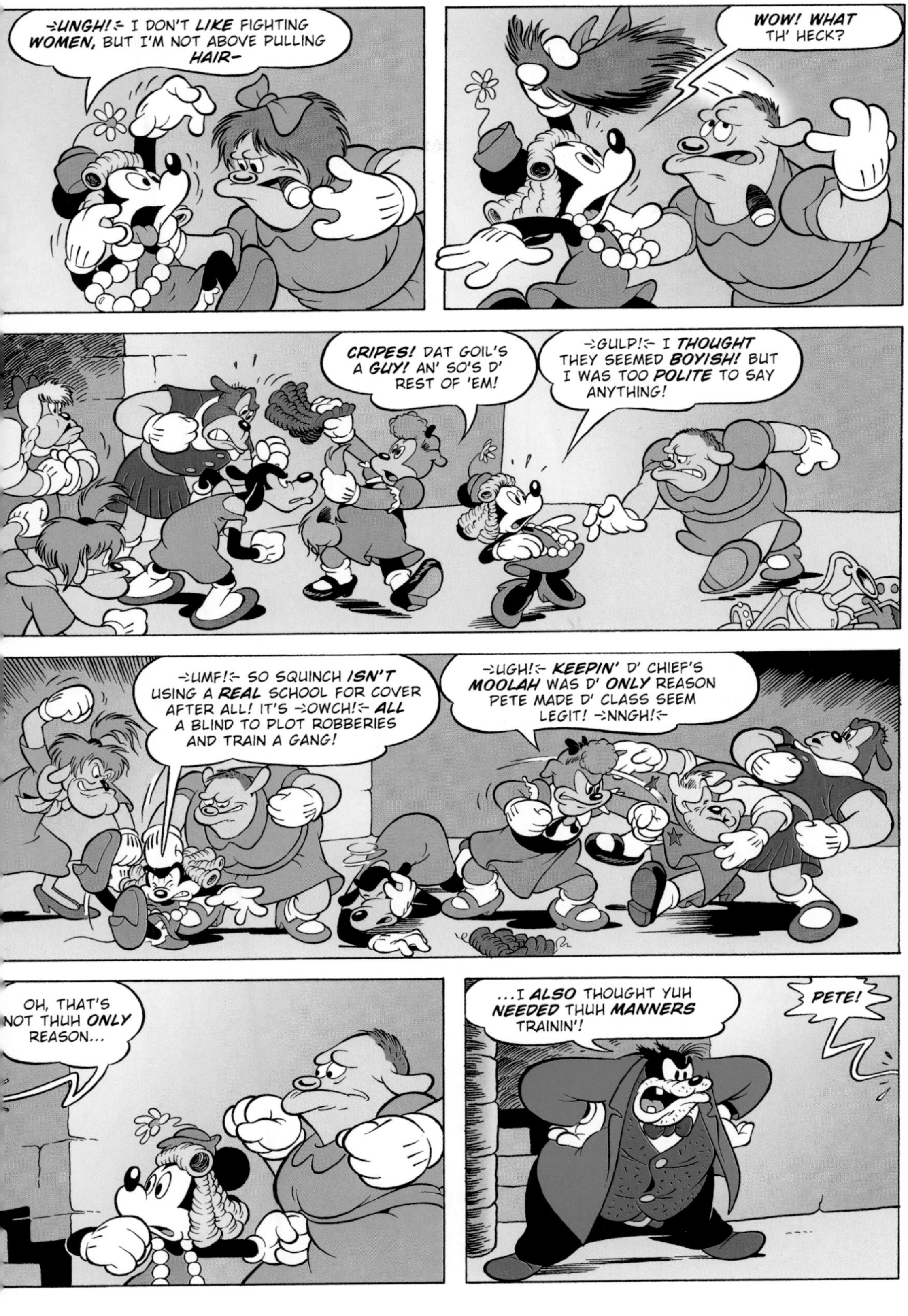

-UNGH!- I DON'T LIKE FIGHTING WOMEN, BUT I'M NOT ABOVE PULLING HAIR-
WOW! WHAT TH' HECK?
CRIPES! DAT GOIL'S A GUY! AN' SO'S D' REST OF 'EM!
-GULP!- I THOUGHT THEY SEEMED BOYISH! BUT I WAS TOO POLITE TO SAY ANYTHING!
-UMF!- SO SQUINCH ISN'T USING A REAL SCHOOL FOR COVER AFTER ALL! IT'S -OWCH!- ALL A BLIND TO PLOT ROBBERIES AND TRAIN A GANG!
-UGH!- KEEPIN' D' CHIEF'S MOOLAH WAS D' ONLY REASON PETE MADE D' CLASS SEEM LEGIT! -NNGH!-
OH, THAT'S NOT THUH ONLY REASON...
...I ALSO THOUGHT YUH NEEDED THUH MANNERS TRAININ'!
PETE!

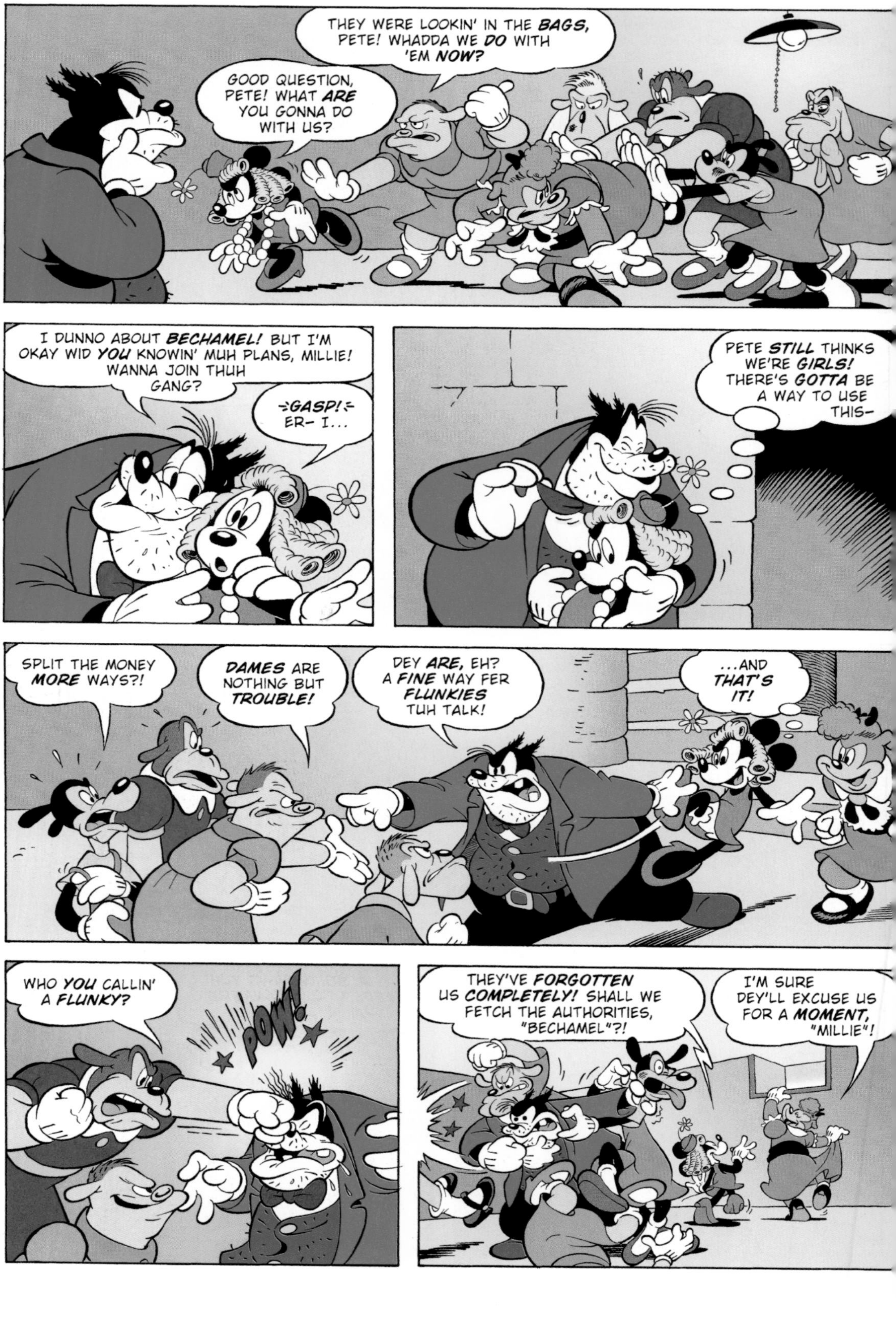
THEY WERE LOOKIN' IN THE BAGS, PETE! WHADDA WE DO WITH 'EM NOW?
GOOD QUESTION, PETE! WHAT ARE YOU GONNA DO WITH US?
I DUNNO ABOUT BECHAMEL! BUT I'M OKAY WID YOU KNOWIN' MUH PLANS, MILLIE! WANNA JOIN THUH GANG?
GASP! ER- I...
PETE STILL THINKS WE'RE GIRLS! THERE'S GOTTA BE A WAY TO USE THIS-
SPLIT THE MONEY MORE WAYS?!
DAMES ARE NOTHING BUT TROUBLE!
DEY ARE, EH? A FINE WAY FER FLUNKIES TUH TALK!
...AND THAT'S IT!
WHO YOU CALLIN' A FLUNKY?
POW!
THEY'VE FORGOTTEN US COMPLETELY! SHALL WE FETCH THE AUTHORITIES, "BECHAMEL"?!
I'M SURE DEY'LL EXCUSE US FOR A MOMENT, "MILLIE"!

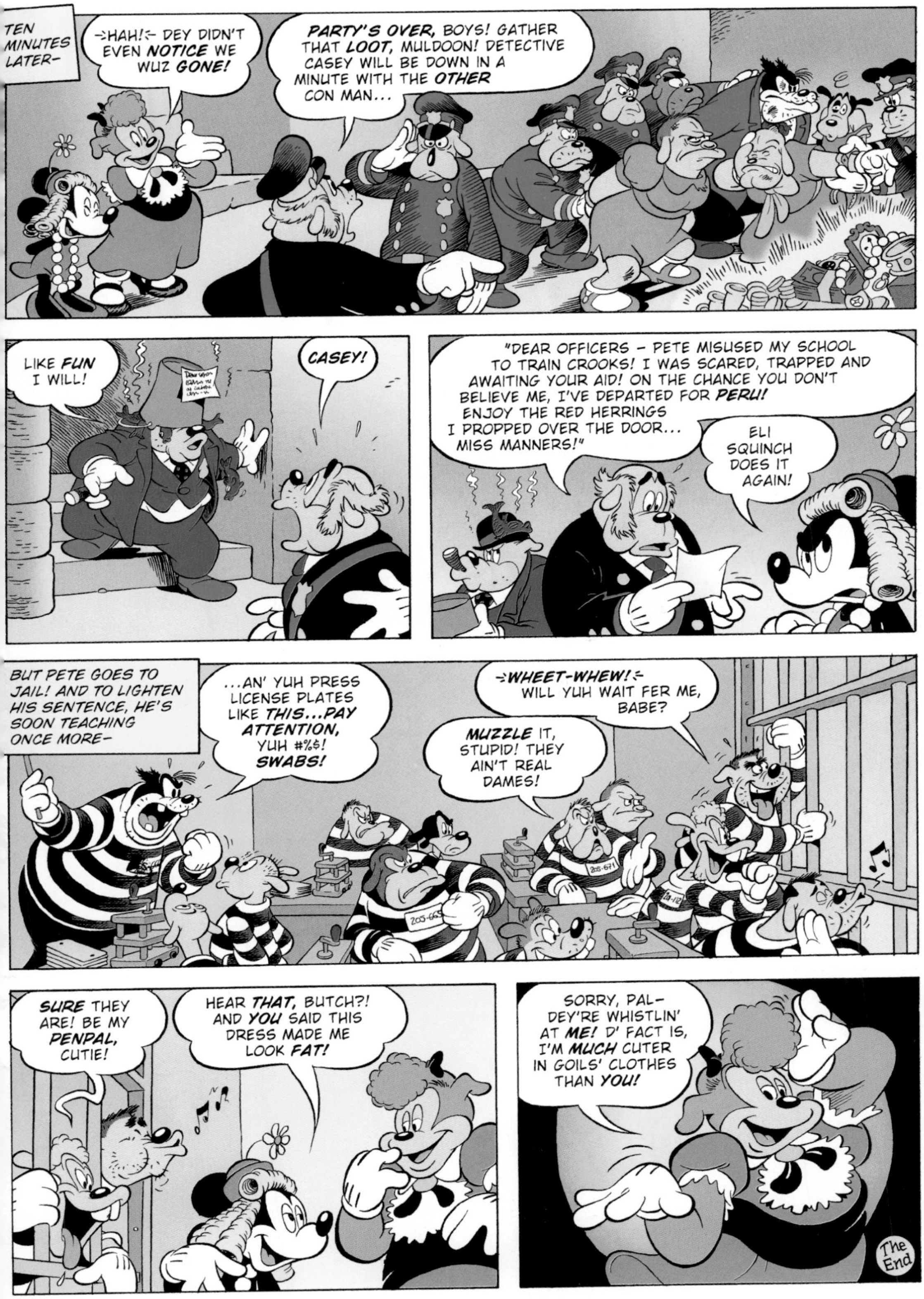
TEN MINUTES LATER–
–HAH!– DEY DIDN'T EVEN NOTICE WE WUZ GONE!
PARTY'S OVER, BOYS! GATHER THAT LOOT, MULDOON! DETECTIVE CASEY WILL BE DOWN IN A MINUTE WITH THE OTHER CON MAN...
LIKE FUN I WILL!
CASEY!
"DEAR OFFICERS – PETE MISUSED MY SCHOOL TO TRAIN CROOKS! I WAS SCARED, TRAPPED AND AWAITING YOUR AID! ON THE CHANCE YOU DON'T BELIEVE ME, I'VE DEPARTED FOR PERU! ENJOY THE RED HERRINGS I PROPPED OVER THE DOOR... MISS MANNERS!"
ELI SQUINCH DOES IT AGAIN!
BUT PETE GOES TO JAIL! AND TO LIGHTEN HIS SENTENCE, HE'S SOON TEACHING ONCE MORE–
...AN' YUH PRESS LICENSE PLATES LIKE THIS...PAY ATTENTION, YUH #%$! SWABS!
–WHEET-WHEW!– WILL YUH WAIT FER ME, BABE?
MUZZLE IT, STUPID! THEY AIN'T REAL DAMES!
SURE THEY ARE! BE MY PENPAL, CUTIE!
HEAR THAT, BUTCH?! AND YOU SAID THIS DRESS MADE ME LOOK FAT!
SORRY, PAL– DEY'RE WHISTLIN' AT ME! D' FACT IS, I'M MUCH CUTER IN GOILS' CLOTHES THAN YOU!
The End

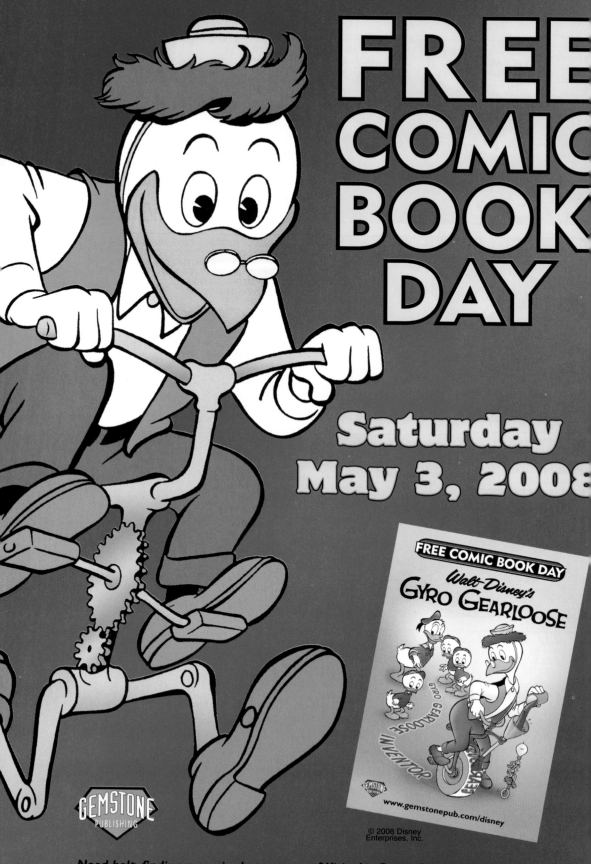

FREE COMIC BOOK DAY

Saturday
May 3, 2008

FREE COMIC BOOK DAY
Walt Disney's
GYRO GEARLOOSE

GYRO GEARLOOSE
INVENTOR

GEMSTONE

www.gemstonepub.com/disney

GEMSTONE
PUBLISHING

© 2008 Disney
Enterprises, Inc.

Need help finding a comic shop near you? Visit the Comic Shop Locator Service
at http://csls.diamondcomics.com or call 1-888-COMIC-BOOK (toll-free)!

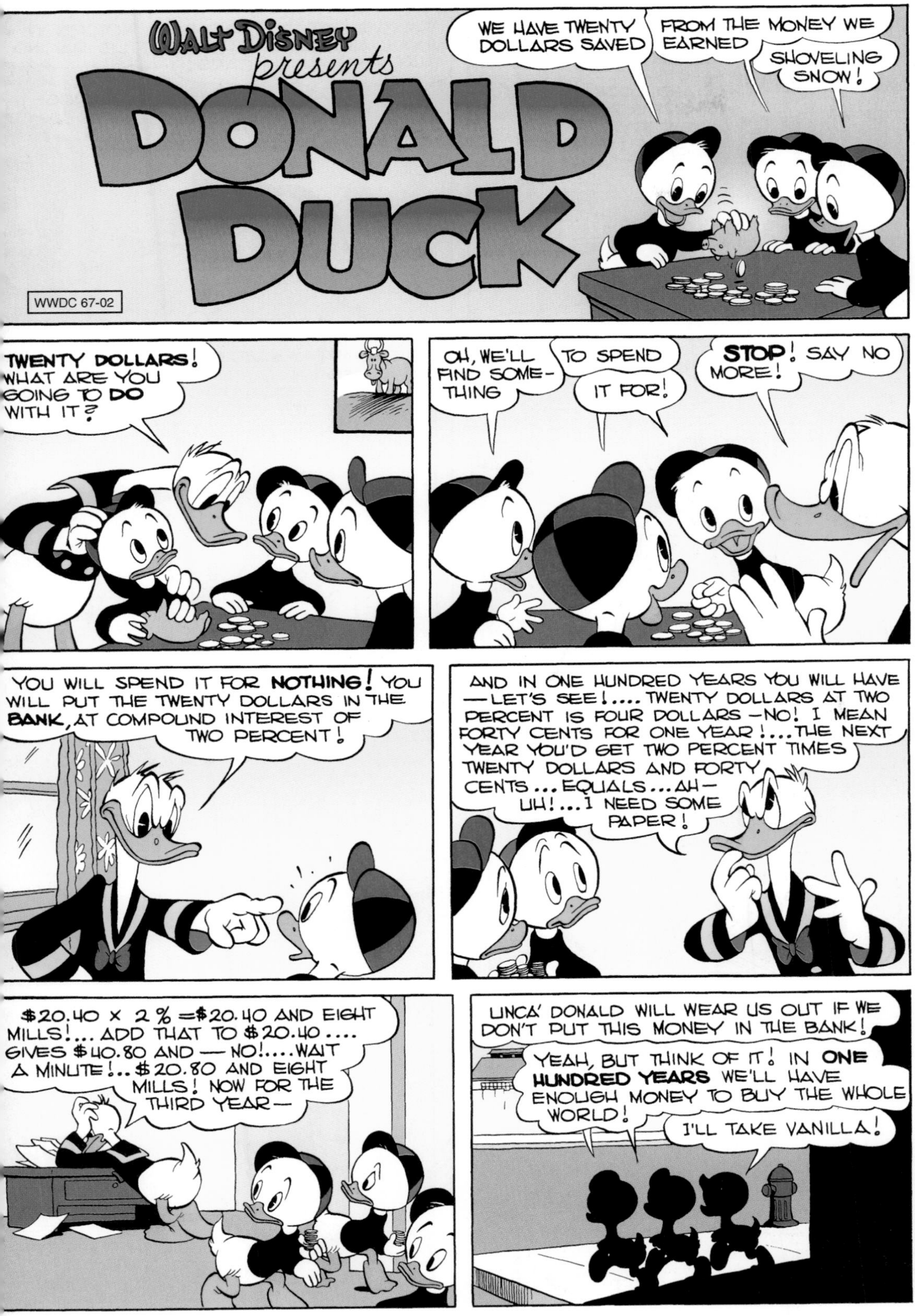
WALT DISNEY presents
DONALD DUCK
WWDC 67-02
WE HAVE TWENTY DOLLARS SAVED
FROM THE MONEY WE EARNED
SHOVELING SNOW!
TWENTY DOLLARS! WHAT ARE YOU GOING TO DO WITH IT?
OH, WE'LL FIND SOMETHING
TO SPEND
IT FOR!
STOP! SAY NO MORE!
YOU WILL SPEND IT FOR NOTHING! YOU WILL PUT THE TWENTY DOLLARS IN THE BANK, AT COMPOUND INTEREST OF TWO PERCENT!
AND IN ONE HUNDRED YEARS YOU WILL HAVE —LET'S SEE!.... TWENTY DOLLARS AT TWO PERCENT IS FOUR DOLLARS —NO! I MEAN FORTY CENTS FOR ONE YEAR!... THE NEXT YEAR YOU'D GET TWO PERCENT TIMES TWENTY DOLLARS AND FORTY CENTS ... EQUALS ... AH— UH!... I NEED SOME PAPER!
$20.40 x 2% =$20.40 AND EIGHT MILLS!... ADD THAT TO $20.40.... GIVES $40.80 AND — NO!.... WAIT A MINUTE!... $20.80 AND EIGHT MILLS! NOW FOR THE THIRD YEAR—
UNCA' DONALD WILL WEAR US OUT IF WE DON'T PUT THIS MONEY IN THE BANK!
YEAH, BUT THINK OF IT! IN ONE HUNDRED YEARS WE'LL HAVE ENOUGH MONEY TO BUY THE WHOLE WORLD!
I'LL TAKE VANILLA!

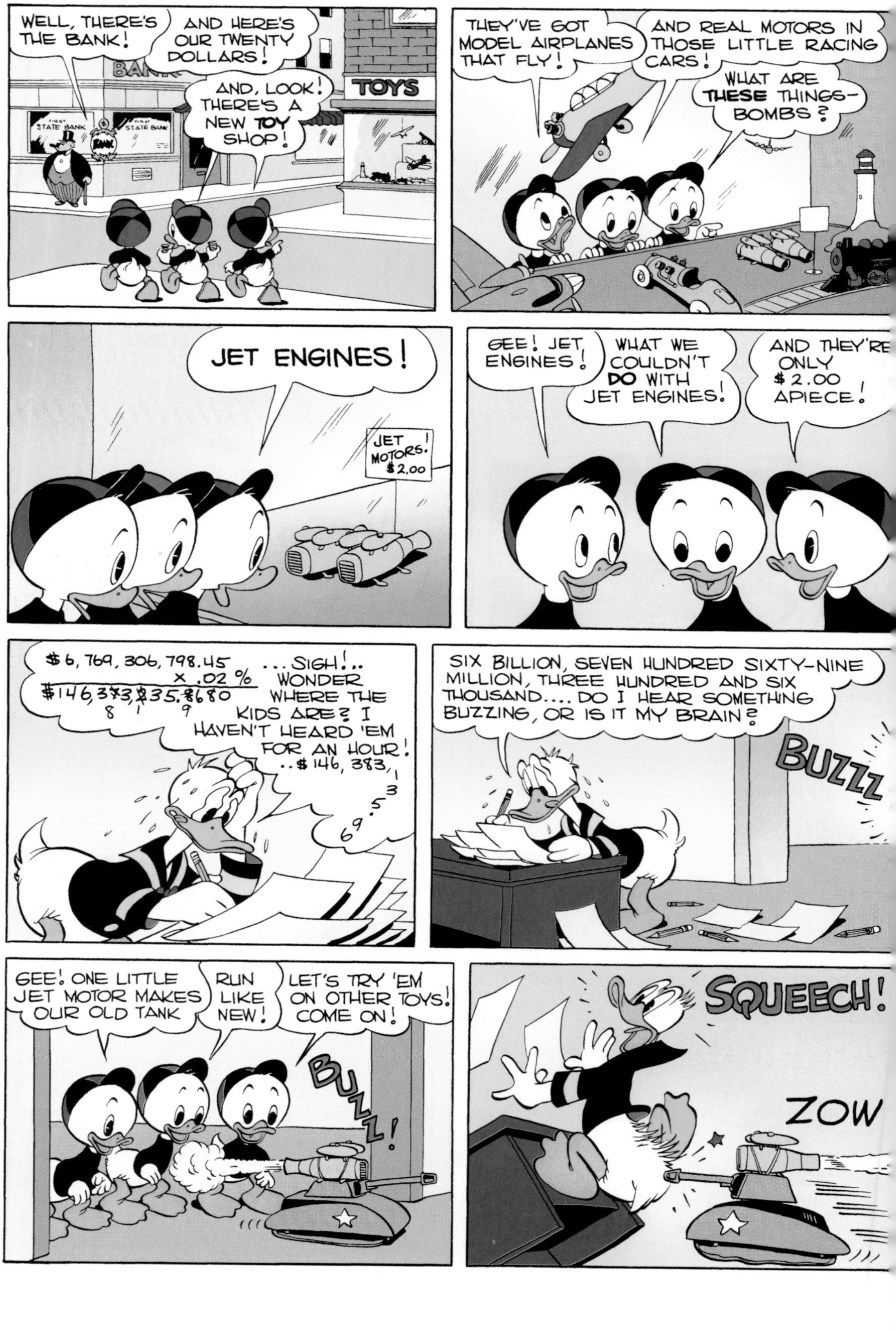
WELL, THERE'S THE BANK!
AND HERE'S OUR TWENTY DOLLARS!
AND, LOOK! THERE'S A NEW TOY SHOP!
TOYS
FIRST STATE BANK
BANK
THEY'VE GOT MODEL AIRPLANES THAT FLY!
AND REAL MOTORS IN THOSE LITTLE RACING CARS!
WHAT ARE THESE THINGS-BOMBS?
JET ENGINES!
JET MOTORS! $2.00
GEE! JET ENGINES!
WHAT WE COULDN'T DO WITH JET ENGINES!
AND THEY'RE ONLY $2.00 APIECE!
$6,769,306,798.45 x .02% $146,373,835.8680
...SIGH!.. WONDER WHERE THE KIDS ARE? I HAVEN'T HEARD 'EM FOR AN HOUR! ..$146,383,
SIX BILLION, SEVEN HUNDRED SIXTY-NINE MILLION, THREE HUNDRED AND SIX THOUSAND.... DO I HEAR SOMETHING BUZZING, OR IS IT MY BRAIN?
BUZZZ
GEE! ONE LITTLE JET MOTOR MAKES OUR OLD TANK
RUN LIKE NEW!
LET'S TRY 'EM ON OTHER TOYS! COME ON!
BUZZZ!
SQUEECH!
ZOW

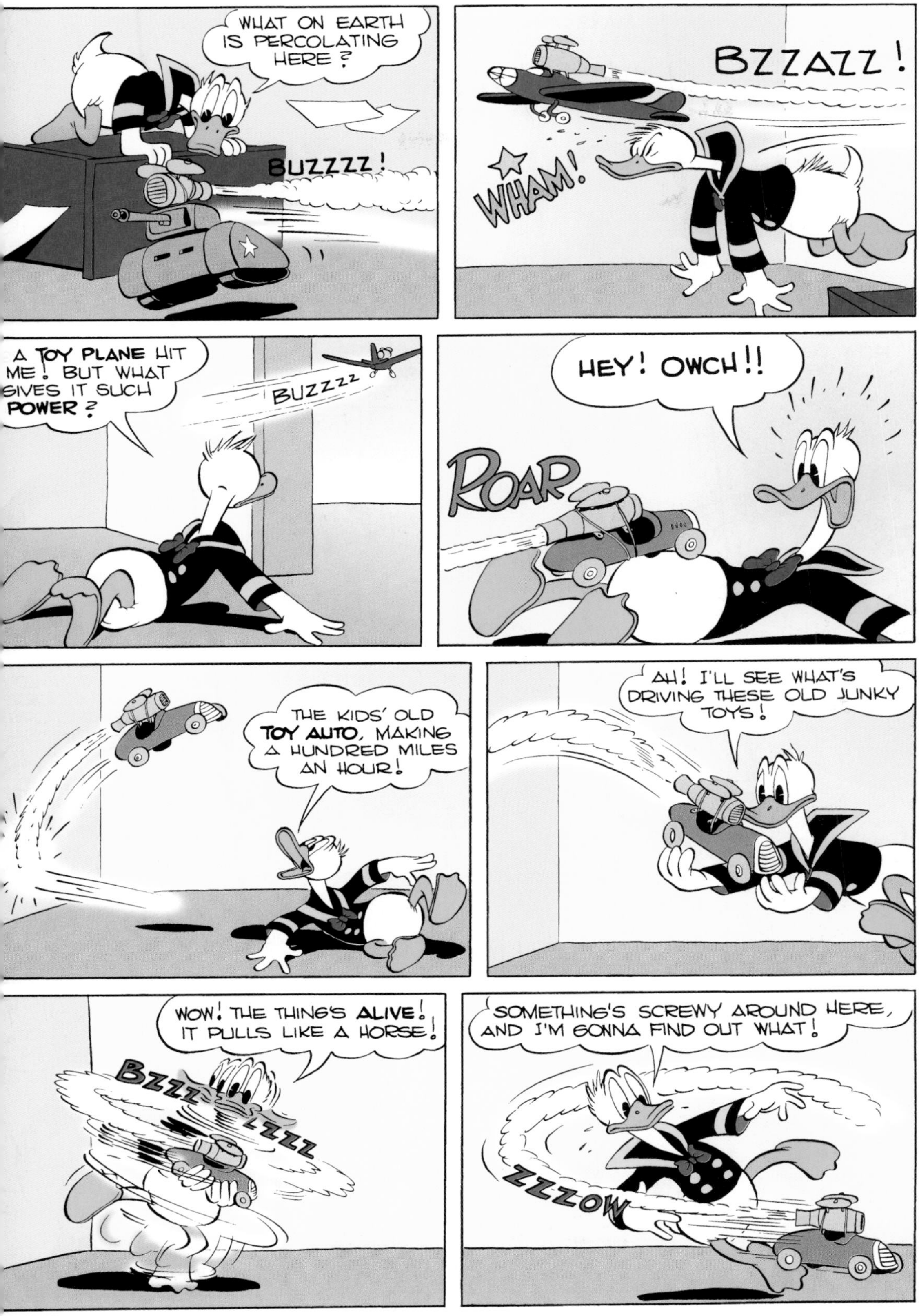
WHAT ON EARTH IS PERCOLATING HERE?
BUZZZZ!
BZZAZZ!
WHAM!
A TOY PLANE HIT ME! BUT WHAT GIVES IT SUCH POWER?
BUZZZZ
HEY! OWCH!!
ROAR
THE KIDS' OLD TOY AUTO, MAKING A HUNDRED MILES AN HOUR!
AH! I'LL SEE WHAT'S DRIVING THESE OLD JUNKY TOYS!
WOW! THE THING'S ALIVE! IT PULLS LIKE A HORSE!
BZZZZZZZZ
SOMETHING'S SCREWY AROUND HERE, AND I'M GONNA FIND OUT WHAT!
ZZZZOW

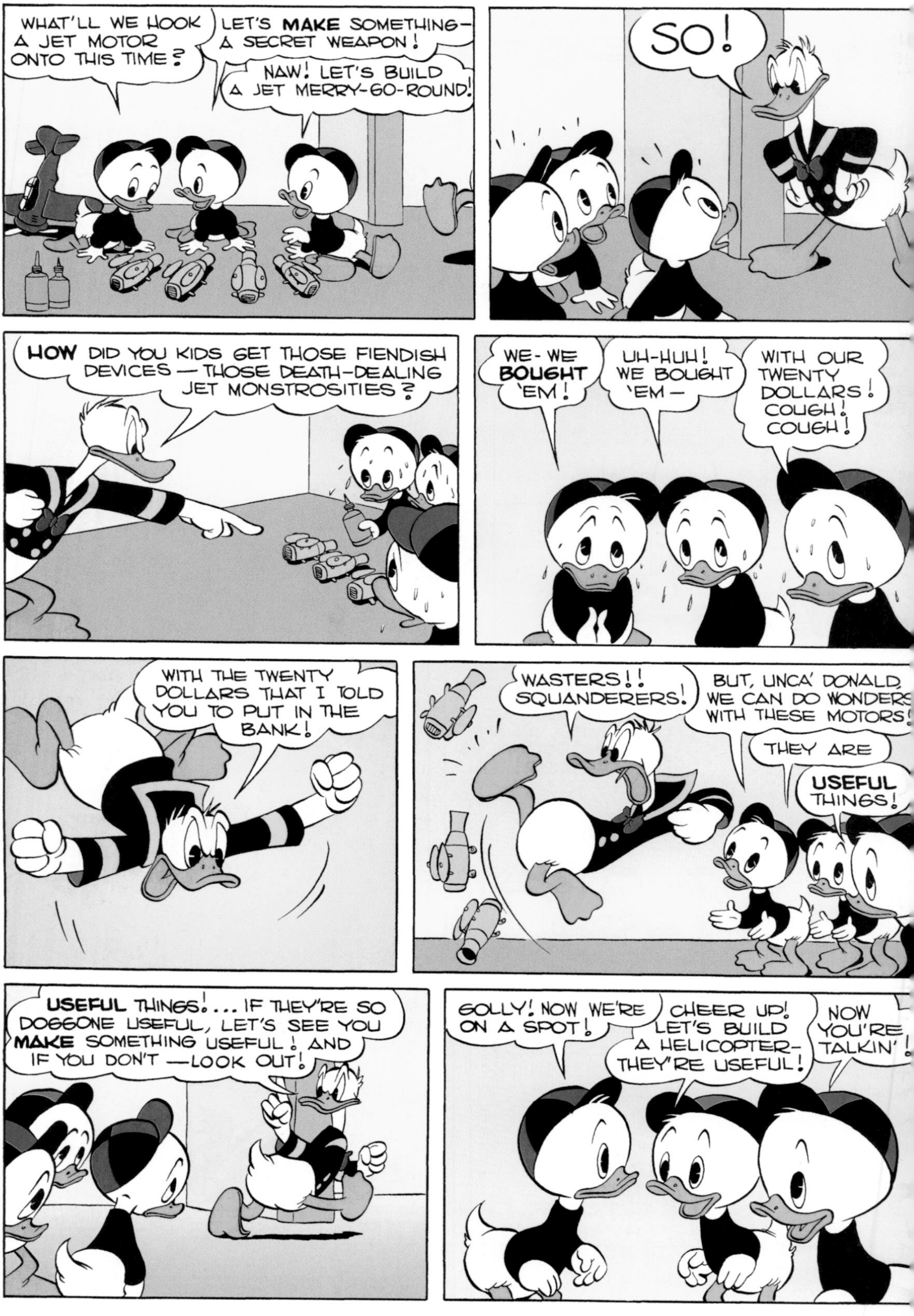
WHAT'LL WE HOOK A JET MOTOR ONTO THIS TIME?
LET'S **MAKE** SOMETHING— A SECRET WEAPON!
NAW! LET'S BUILD A JET MERRY-GO-ROUND!
SO!
HOW DID YOU KIDS GET THOSE FIENDISH DEVICES — THOSE DEATH-DEALING JET MONSTROSITIES?
WE- WE **BOUGHT** 'EM!
UH-HUH! WE BOUGHT 'EM —
WITH OUR TWENTY DOLLARS! COUGH! COUGH!
WITH THE TWENTY DOLLARS THAT I TOLD YOU TO PUT IN THE BANK!
WASTERS!! SQUANDERERS!
BUT, UNCA' DONALD, WE CAN DO WONDERS WITH THESE MOTORS!
THEY ARE
USEFUL THINGS!
USEFUL THINGS!... IF THEY'RE SO DOGGONE USEFUL, LET'S SEE YOU **MAKE** SOMETHING USEFUL! AND IF YOU DON'T —LOOK OUT!
GOLLY! NOW WE'RE ON A SPOT!
CHEER UP! LET'S BUILD A HELICOPTER— THEY'RE USEFUL!
NOW YOU'RE TALKIN'!

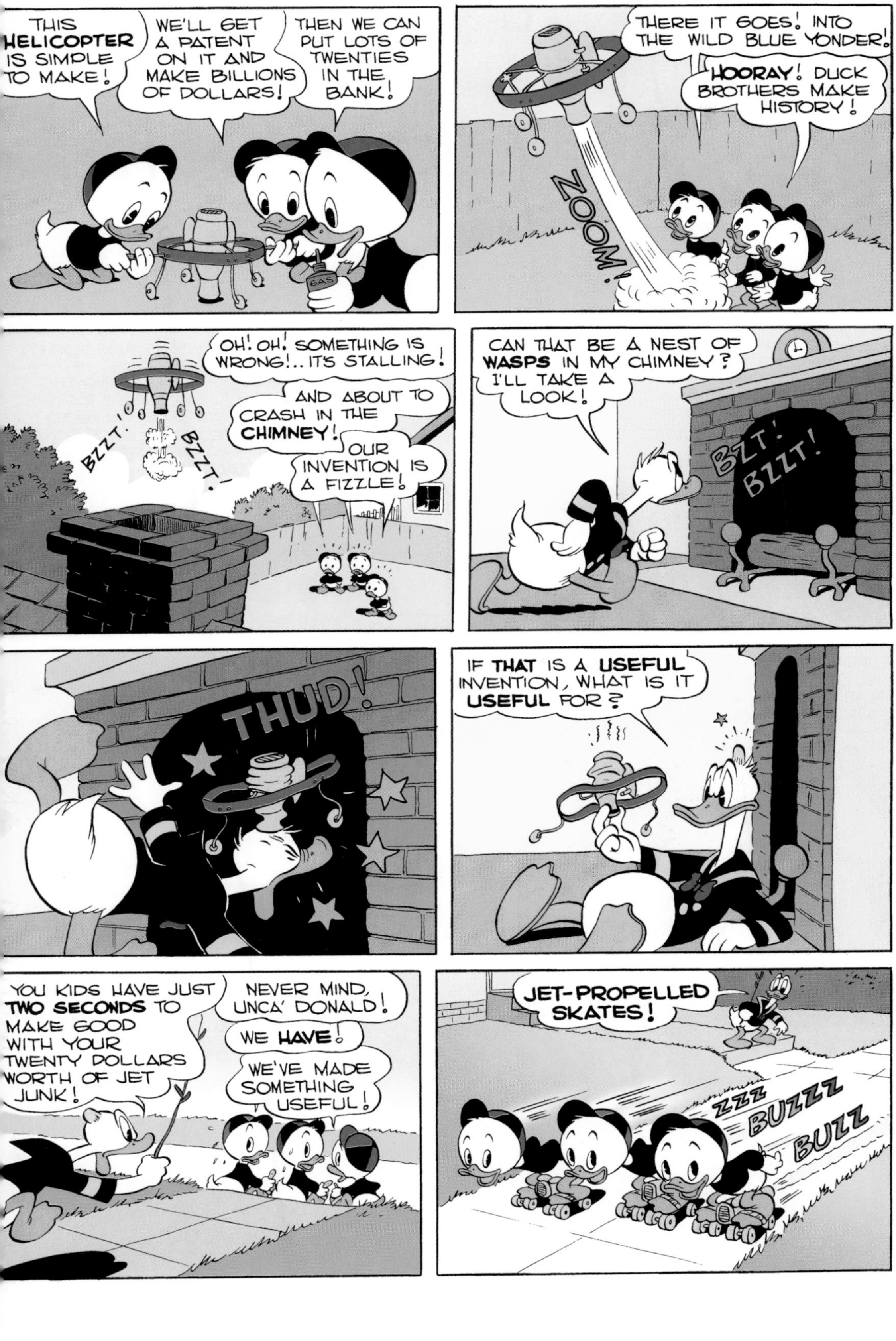

THIS **HELICOPTER** IS SIMPLE TO MAKE!
WE'LL GET A PATENT ON IT AND MAKE BILLIONS OF DOLLARS!
THEN WE CAN PUT LOTS OF TWENTIES IN THE BANK!
GAS
THERE IT GOES! INTO THE WILD BLUE YONDER!
HOORAY! DUCK BROTHERS MAKE HISTORY!
ZOOM!
OH! OH! SOMETHING IS WRONG!.. IT'S STALLING!
AND ABOUT TO CRASH IN THE **CHIMNEY**!
OUR INVENTION IS A FIZZLE!
BZZT!
BZZT!
CAN THAT BE A NEST OF **WASPS** IN MY CHIMNEY? I'LL TAKE A LOOK!
BZZT! BZZT!
THUD!
IF **THAT** IS A **USEFUL** INVENTION, WHAT IS IT **USEFUL** FOR?
YOU KIDS HAVE JUST **TWO SECONDS** TO MAKE GOOD WITH YOUR TWENTY DOLLARS WORTH OF JET JUNK!
NEVER MIND, UNCA' DONALD!
WE **HAVE**!
WE'VE MADE SOMETHING USEFUL!
JET-PROPELLED SKATES!
ZZZ
BUZZZ
BUZZ

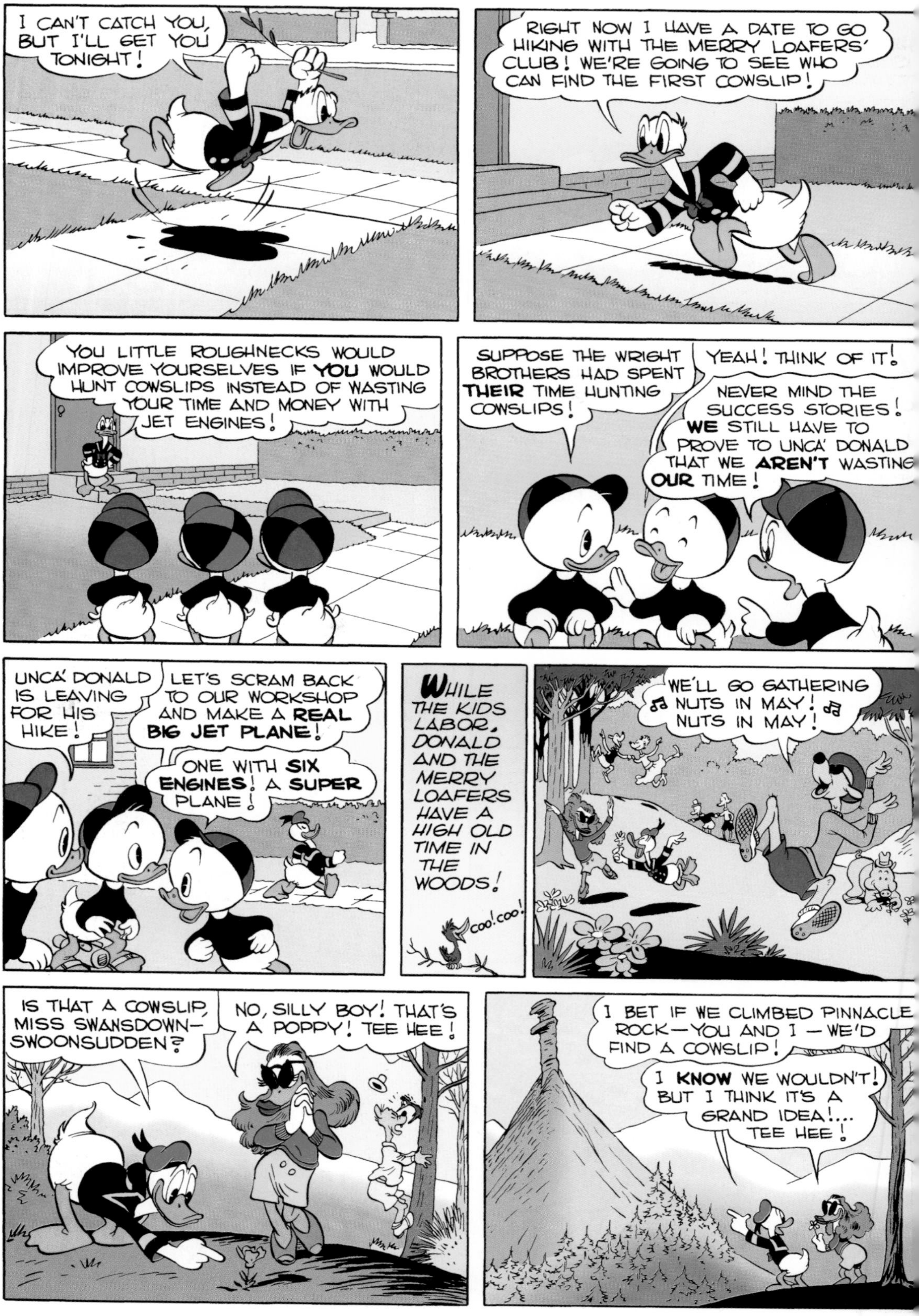
I CAN'T CATCH YOU, BUT I'LL GET YOU TONIGHT!
RIGHT NOW I HAVE A DATE TO GO HIKING WITH THE MERRY LOAFERS' CLUB! WE'RE GOING TO SEE WHO CAN FIND THE FIRST COWSLIP!
YOU LITTLE ROUGHNECKS WOULD IMPROVE YOURSELVES IF **YOU** WOULD HUNT COWSLIPS INSTEAD OF WASTING YOUR TIME AND MONEY WITH JET ENGINES!
SUPPOSE THE WRIGHT BROTHERS HAD SPENT **THEIR** TIME HUNTING COWSLIPS!
YEAH! THINK OF IT!
NEVER MIND THE SUCCESS STORIES! **WE** STILL HAVE TO PROVE TO UNCA' DONALD THAT WE **AREN'T** WASTING **OUR** TIME!
UNCA' DONALD IS LEAVING FOR HIS HIKE!
LET'S SCRAM BACK TO OUR WORKSHOP AND MAKE A **REAL BIG JET PLANE**!
ONE WITH **SIX ENGINES**! A **SUPER** PLANE!
WHILE THE KIDS LABOR, DONALD AND THE MERRY LOAFERS HAVE A HIGH OLD TIME IN THE WOODS!
COO! COO!
WE'LL GO GATHERING NUTS IN MAY! NUTS IN MAY!
IS THAT A COWSLIP, MISS SWANSDOWN-SWOONSUDDEN?
NO, SILLY BOY! THAT'S A POPPY! TEE HEE!
I BET IF WE CLIMBED PINNACLE ROCK—YOU AND I—WE'D FIND A COWSLIP!
I **KNOW** WE WOULDN'T! BUT I THINK IT'S A GRAND IDEA!... TEE HEE!

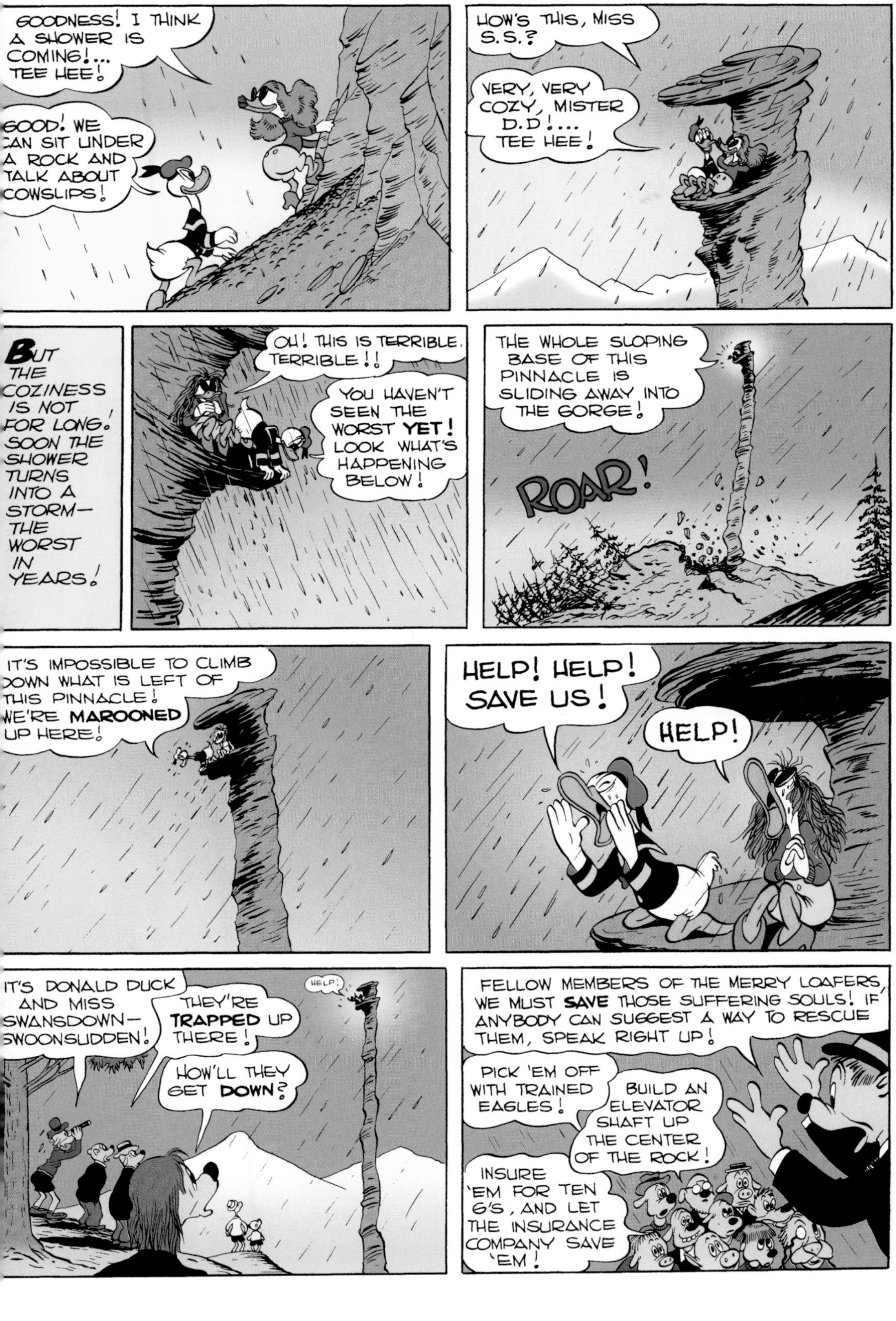
GOODNESS! I THINK A SHOWER IS COMING!... TEE HEE!
GOOD! WE CAN SIT UNDER A ROCK AND TALK ABOUT COWSLIPS!
HOW'S THIS, MISS S.S.?
VERY, VERY COZY, MISTER D.D!... TEE HEE!
BUT THE COZINESS IS NOT FOR LONG. SOON THE SHOWER TURNS INTO A STORM—THE WORST IN YEARS!
OH! THIS IS TERRIBLE, TERRIBLE!!
YOU HAVEN'T SEEN THE WORST YET! LOOK WHAT'S HAPPENING BELOW!
THE WHOLE SLOPING BASE OF THIS PINNACLE IS SLIDING AWAY INTO THE GORGE!
ROAR!
IT'S IMPOSSIBLE TO CLIMB DOWN WHAT IS LEFT OF THIS PINNACLE! WE'RE MAROONED UP HERE!
HELP! HELP! SAVE US!
HELP!
IT'S DONALD DUCK AND MISS SWANSDOWN-SWOONSUDDEN!
HELP!
THEY'RE TRAPPED UP THERE!
HOW'LL THEY GET DOWN?
FELLOW MEMBERS OF THE MERRY LOAFERS, WE MUST SAVE THOSE SUFFERING SOULS! IF ANYBODY CAN SUGGEST A WAY TO RESCUE THEM, SPEAK RIGHT UP!
PICK 'EM OFF WITH TRAINED EAGLES!
BUILD AN ELEVATOR SHAFT UP THE CENTER OF THE ROCK!
INSURE 'EM FOR TEN G'S, AND LET THE INSURANCE COMPANY SAVE 'EM!

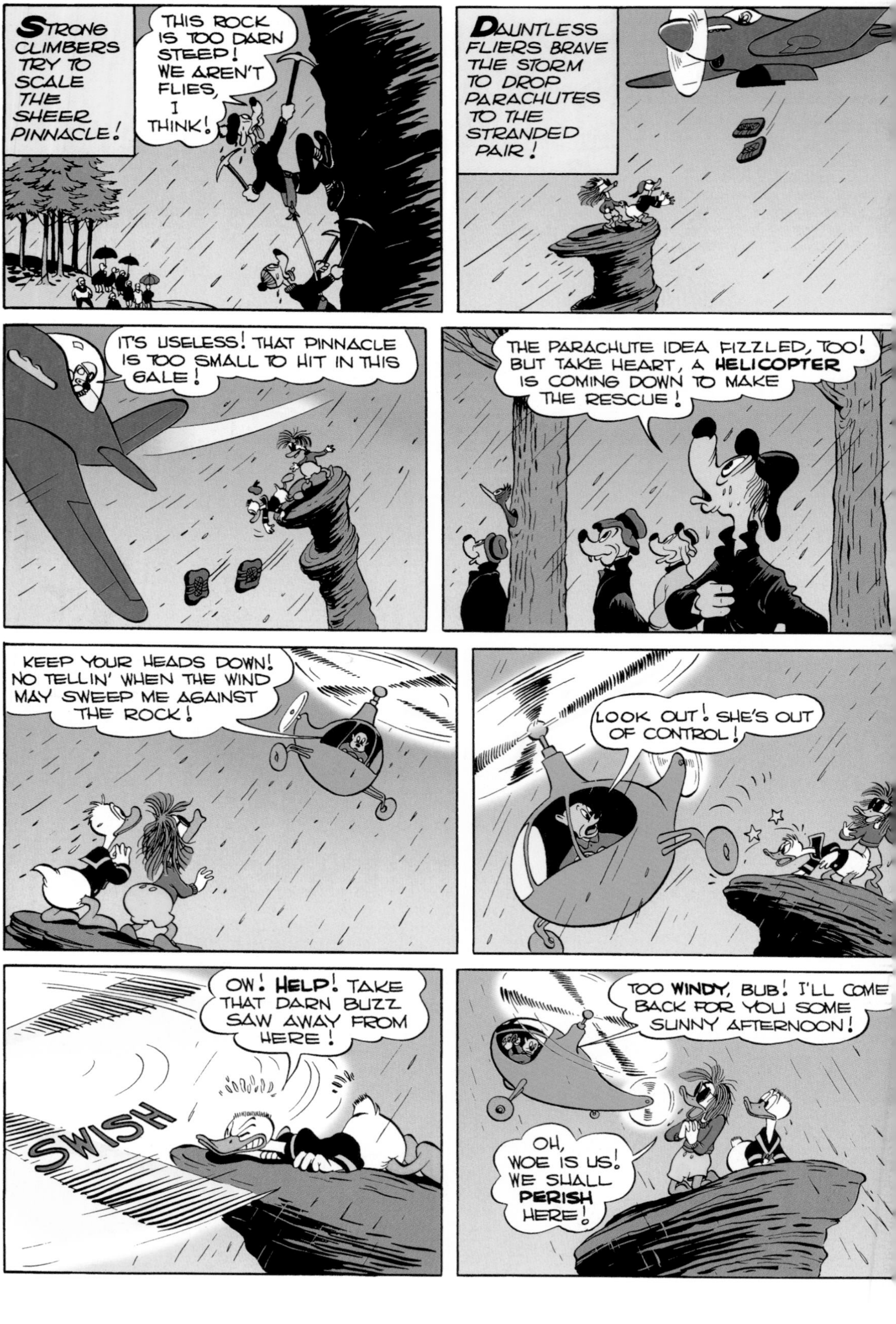
STRONG CLIMBERS TRY TO SCALE THE SHEER PINNACLE!
THIS ROCK IS TOO DARN STEEP! WE AREN'T FLIES, I THINK!
DAUNTLESS FLIERS BRAVE THE STORM TO DROP PARACHUTES TO THE STRANDED PAIR!
IT'S USELESS! THAT PINNACLE IS TOO SMALL TO HIT IN THIS GALE!
THE PARACHUTE IDEA FIZZLED, TOO! BUT TAKE HEART, A HELICOPTER IS COMING DOWN TO MAKE THE RESCUE!
KEEP YOUR HEADS DOWN! NO TELLIN' WHEN THE WIND MAY SWEEP ME AGAINST THE ROCK!
LOOK OUT! SHE'S OUT OF CONTROL!
OW! HELP! TAKE THAT DARN BUZZ SAW AWAY FROM HERE!
SWISH
TOO WINDY, BUB! I'LL COME BACK FOR YOU SOME SUNNY AFTERNOON!
OH, WOE IS US! WE SHALL PERISH HERE!

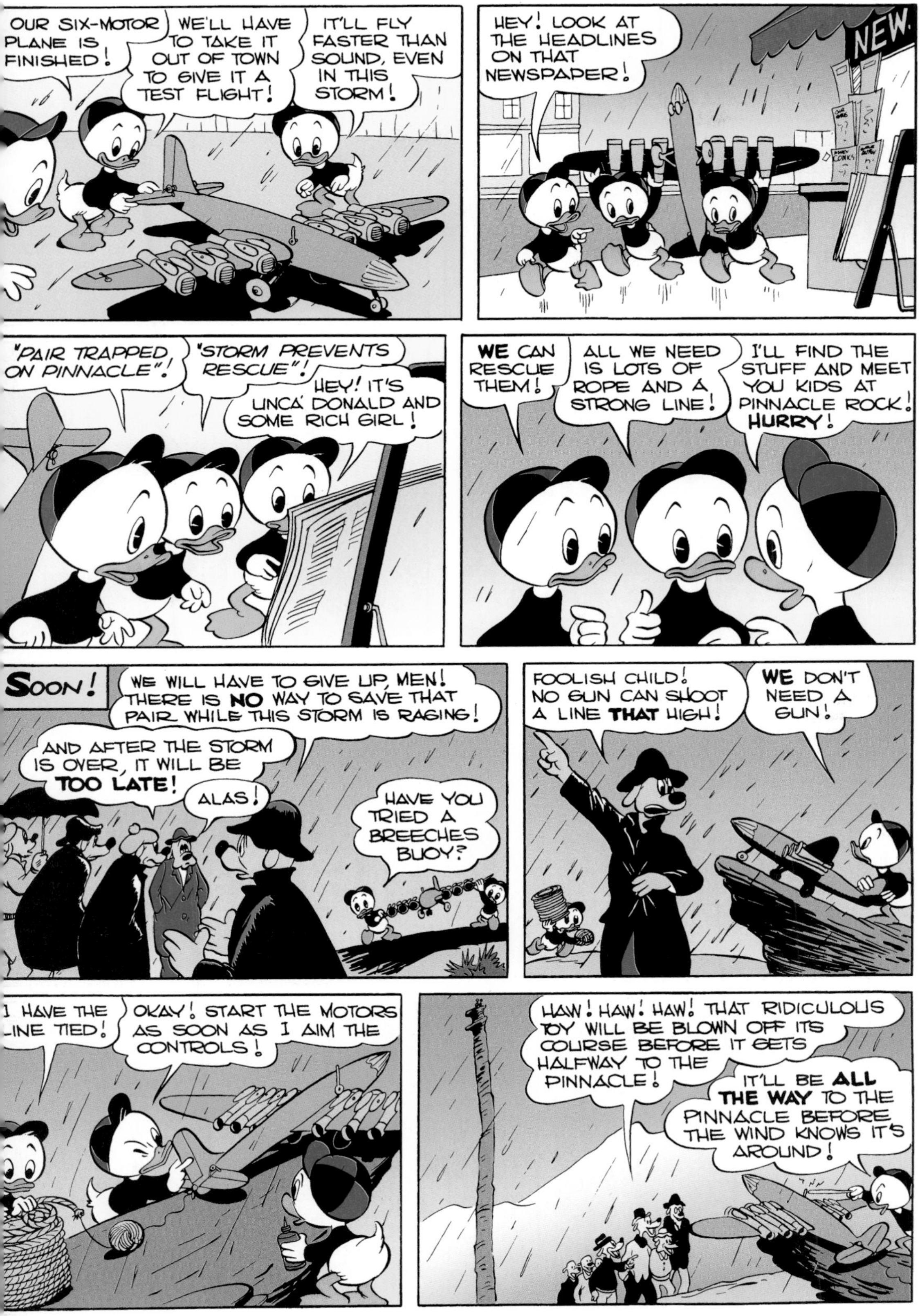

OUR SIX-MOTOR PLANE IS FINISHED!
WE'LL HAVE TO TAKE IT OUT OF TOWN TO GIVE IT A TEST FLIGHT!
IT'LL FLY FASTER THAN SOUND, EVEN IN THIS STORM!
HEY! LOOK AT THE HEADLINES ON THAT NEWSPAPER!
NEW
"PAIR TRAPPED ON PINNACLE"!
"STORM PREVENTS RESCUE"!
HEY! IT'S UNCA' DONALD AND SOME RICH GIRL!
WE CAN RESCUE THEM!
ALL WE NEED IS LOTS OF ROPE AND A STRONG LINE!
I'LL FIND THE STUFF AND MEET YOU KIDS AT PINNACLE ROCK! HURRY!
SOON!
WE WILL HAVE TO GIVE UP, MEN! THERE IS NO WAY TO SAVE THAT PAIR WHILE THIS STORM IS RAGING!
AND AFTER THE STORM IS OVER, IT WILL BE TOO LATE!
ALAS!
HAVE YOU TRIED A BREECHES BUOY?
FOOLISH CHILD! NO GUN CAN SHOOT A LINE THAT HIGH!
WE DON'T NEED A GUN!
I HAVE THE LINE TIED!
OKAY! START THE MOTORS AS SOON AS I AIM THE CONTROLS!
HAW! HAW! HAW! THAT RIDICULOUS TOY WILL BE BLOWN OFF ITS COURSE BEFORE IT GETS HALFWAY TO THE PINNACLE!
IT'LL BE ALL THE WAY TO THE PINNACLE BEFORE THE WIND KNOWS IT'S AROUND!

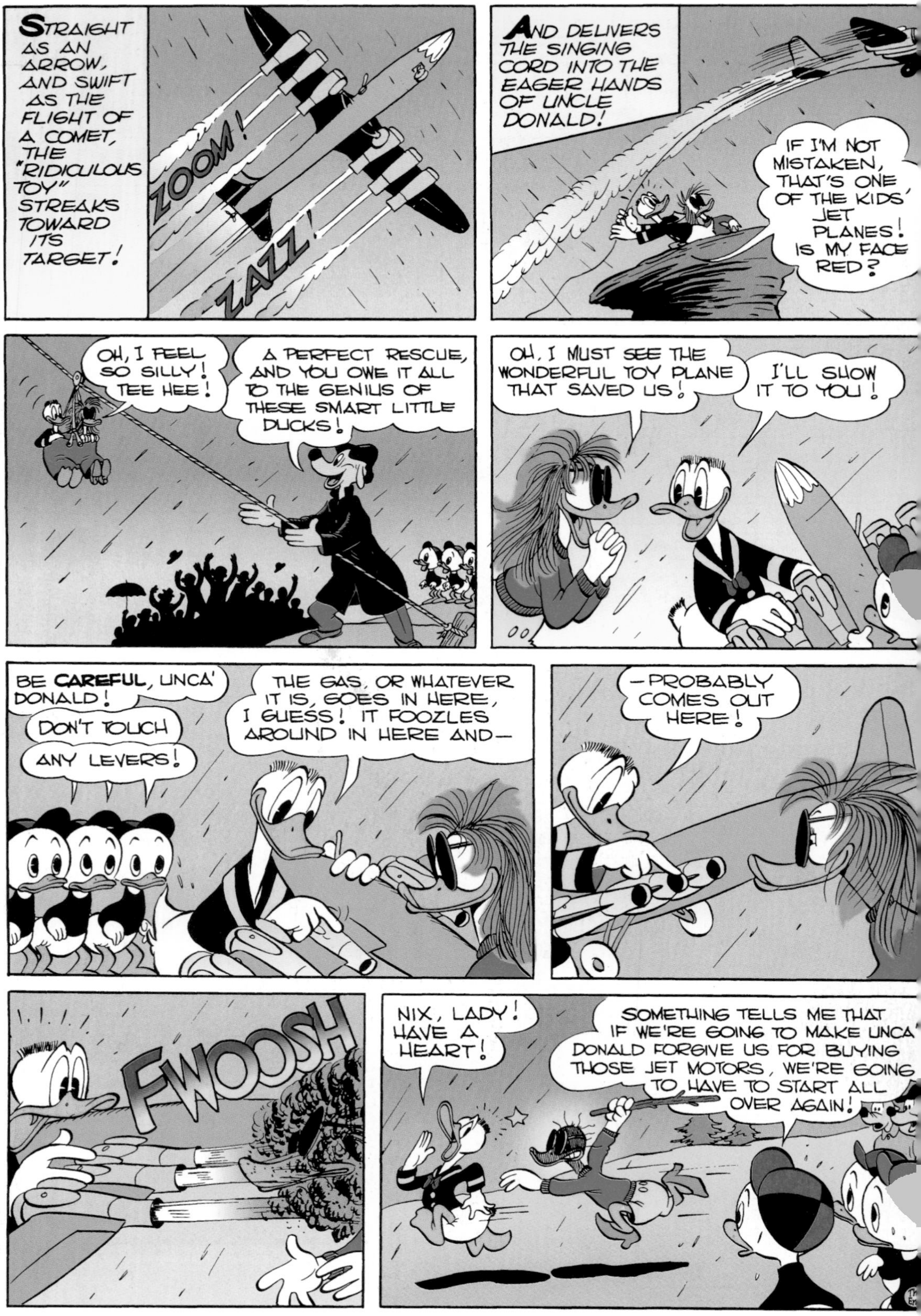

STRAIGHT AS AN ARROW, AND SWIFT AS THE FLIGHT OF A COMET, THE "RIDICULOUS TOY" STREAKS TOWARD ITS TARGET!
ZOOM!
ZAZZ!
AND DELIVERS THE SINGING CORD INTO THE EAGER HANDS OF UNCLE DONALD!
IF I'M NOT MISTAKEN, THAT'S ONE OF THE KIDS' JET PLANES! IS MY FACE RED?
OH, I FEEL SO SILLY! TEE HEE!
A PERFECT RESCUE, AND YOU OWE IT ALL TO THE GENIUS OF THESE SMART LITTLE DUCKS!
OH, I MUST SEE THE WONDERFUL TOY PLANE THAT SAVED US!
I'LL SHOW IT TO YOU!
BE CAREFUL, UNCA' DONALD!
DON'T TOUCH
ANY LEVERS!
THE GAS, OR WHATEVER IT IS, GOES IN HERE, I GUESS! IT FOOZLES AROUND IN HERE AND—
—PROBABLY COMES OUT HERE!
FWOOSH
NIX, LADY! HAVE A HEART!
SOMETHING TELLS ME THAT IF WE'RE GOING TO MAKE UNCA' DONALD FORGIVE US FOR BUYING THOSE JET MOTORS, WE'RE GOING TO HAVE TO START ALL OVER AGAIN!